W9-CBC-551

Gracefully Grayson

Gracefully Grayson

Ami Polonsky

HYPERION
LOS ANGELES ☆ NEW YORK

 For information address Hyperion, 125 West End Avenue, New York, New York 10023.

First Edition
10 9 8 7 6 5 4 3 2 1
G475-5664-5-14227
Printed in the United States of America

Library of Congress Cataloging-in-Publication Data
Polonsky, Ami.
Gracefully Grayson / Ami Polonsky.
pages cm
Summary: "Grayson, a transgender twelve-year-old, learns to accept her true identity and share it with the world"—Provided by publisher.
ISBN 978-1-4231-8527-7—ISBN 1-4231-8527-7
[1. Transgender people—Fiction. 2. Middle schools—Fiction. 3. Schools—Fiction. 4. Theater—Fiction. 5. Self-acceptance—Fiction. 6. Orphans—Fiction. 7. Family life—Fiction.] I. Title.
PZ7.P7687Gr 2014
[Fic]—dc23 2014010155

Reinforced binding
Visit www.un-requiredreading.com

THIS LABEL APPLIES TO TEXT STOCK

For Ben and Ella,
who have great faith in stories

Part One

Chapter 1

IF YOU DRAW a triangle with a circle resting on the top point, nobody will be able to tell that it's a girl in a dress. To add hair, draw kind of a semicircle on top. If you do this, you'll be safe, because it looks like you're just doodling shapes.

I was in third grade when I realized I could draw princesses without anyone knowing and, for more than three years, I've been sketching the same thing in the margins of my notebooks at school. I look up at the board. Mr. Finnegan has already given us almost an entire page of notes, more than most teachers, but I don't mind. Humanities is the best class of the day, and besides, it's no problem for me to take notes and draw at the same time. I sketch another triangle dress in my notebook, circle on the top point, thin semicircle of hair. I try to look at it like I've never seen it before just to *confirm* that nobody else would know that the sketch is really a princess. But I'm good. It's too abstract.

My pen is a glitter pen—silver. I have a gold one in my backpack, but I always leave the purple and pink ones in my drawer at home with the rest of my art supplies. If anyone asks, I can always say I found the silver and gold ones on the floor in the gym or something, but probably nobody will. I want to fill in the dress with the shining silver, add big eyes and a smile and long shimmering hair, but I never would because that's not what boys are supposed to do. I squeeze my eyes almost shut to try to see the princess the way I want to. All I can see is her silver outline, though, so I rest my head in my hand and look out the window instead.

Outside, a giant truck barrels down the street and a city bus honks as it turns the corner. Mrs. Frank, the gym teacher, is bringing some little kids out to the soccer field. They're skipping and running across the grass. Beyond them is Chicago's skyline. Even though the leaves are starting to change color, it still feels like summer, and it's way too hot in the classroom. My bright yellow basketball pants are sticking to my thighs. I push my bangs to the side as I adjust the sweatband on my forehead.

Finn is awesome, and I'm lucky I got him for Humanities, especially since Mrs. Tell is the other humanities teacher and she's probably ninety years old and supposedly horrible. My cousin Jack had her last year and was always in trouble in her class. He blamed it on how boring she was, but lately he's in trouble in every class, and most of what he says these days is bull.

I look back to my notebook as Finn asks Anthony to read a paragraph about the Holocaust aloud. I think of my drawing pads at home, in my top desk drawer. Usually I draw the castles and landscapes huge and then make the people tiny, so they're barely noticeable—the queen, the king, and the little blond princess. When I was younger, my mom was an artist, and I wonder for the millionth time what she would have thought of those drawings and of the sketches in my notebooks at school, and I wonder what she drew when she was my age. The one painting that she left behind especially for me is of the earth surrounded by a wave of trees and sprinkled with smiling animals. Behind the earth is the sky, brightening from darkness into light, and at the top of the sky, one bird that's red, yellow, and blue is soaring, all alone. The painting hangs on the wall next to my bed, so I fall asleep each night looking at it, especially at the bird. And I wake up to it every morning.

Finn writes the names of some places in Europe on the board. I turn to a clean page. "We're going to start talking about people in specific cities who risked their lives to help Jews escape the Nazis," Finn says. He sits on his desk as he waits for us to finish writing.

I look up at him when I'm done. He looks relaxed, as usual. His white dress shirt is tucked neatly into his dark jeans, and he's holding a red dry-erase marker in his hand. "These people had to keep their involvement in the Resistance *secret*." He emphasizes the word by walking back to the board to write it above the other notes.

I doodle a new princess and sketch a jagged circle around her. "How would it feel to hide an enormous, important, life-threatening secret from your friends, your neighbors, and maybe even members of your own family?" Finn continues. I bend down and take my gold glitter pen out of my backpack. His question makes me forget all about the Holocaust and think, instead, of when we were in elementary school, back when we had recess every day, and how, for so many years, I sat on the side steps alone, watching everyone else play. I draw a ring of gold flames outside of the jagged circle. They surround the princess. She suffocates.

The clock ticks on the wall, and somebody coughs behind me. Otherwise, the class is still.

"Grayson? Any thoughts?" Finn finally asks. He usually calls on me if nobody answers; I guess because I can always come up with something to say. "What do you think?" he goes on. "How would you feel if you were going about your life, day to day, all the while hiding a dangerous secret?"

I try to seem calm, like I usually feel in Humanities, but my heart is starting to race. I hesitate and look down at my notes. "I mean, I guess I'd feel like it would be safer to stay away from other people," I finally stumble. Finn waits for me to say more, but I'm kind of hoping he'll call on someone else now.

"Can you elaborate?" he asks.

I adjust my sweatband again. It's damp. "Well," I say, "I'd just stay away from people because I'd be worried I'd accidentally tell them my secret." It sounds like a question, the way I say it. I feel my ears turning red, and I flatten down my hair to hide them.

The class is quiet, and I look down at my glitter pens. The pause feels like forever.

"Okay," Finn finally says slowly. Then he's silent for another second. "Interesting. Does anyone have any thoughts on Grayson's comment?"

I avoid his eyes and glance around the room at the faces I've known pretty much since kindergarten. For a minute, I only look at things, not the people, like the thin braid hanging down the side of Hailey's head that's clasped at the bottom with one of those tiny heart clips, Meagan's pink backpack on the floor next to her desk, the shining wooden desktops.

Then I let my brain adjust and I examine the people. Ryan, who is a complete jerk, sits right across the aisle from me. He glances in my direction, and I look away. On the other side of me, Lila is twirling her long, brown hair into a bun. She seems quiet, but she's completely in charge of the girls. My eyes rest on Amelia, who started at Porter last week. She looks like she belongs in high school, not sixth grade. Her long, reddish hair hangs over her huge chest. Slowly, she puts her hand up.

She seems nervous, and I feel kind of bad for her. It's probably not easy to move once the school year has already started, and especially not to a school like Porter, where most of us are lifers.

"I'd actually make friends with more and more people," she

says sort of softly when Finn calls on her. "I wouldn't stay away from people, because that might look suspicious. I'd just try to act normal, you know, like everyone else." Her pale, freckled cheeks look pink.

"So," Finn says, "on one hand we have Grayson's idea to isolate oneself, and on the other hand is Amelia's idea to surround oneself with lots of people in order not to appear suspicious." Next to the word *secret*, he writes *Isolate v. Integrate* in quick, slanted writing.

I look up at the clock. It's almost time to go, and I can't wait to get to my next class. I copy the last notes quickly. The bell rings, and I stand up with everyone else. "We'll pick up here tomorrow," Finn yells over the sound of rustling notebooks. He glances my way. I concentrate on my shoes as I walk to the door.

Chapter 2

WHEN SCHOOL IS OVER, I get out of the building fast, like I always do. Lots of kids stay after for activities or sports, but I never have. When I was younger, Uncle Evan, Aunt Sally, and my teachers always tried to get me to join debate or the boys' chorus or whatever, but finally they gave up and left me alone. I didn't feel like debating anything in front of an audience, and, even though I have a pretty good voice, I *definitely* wasn't trying out for the boys' chorus.

I look around as I walk to the bus stop. The streets are empty, and it's pretty quiet outside of school. I relax. Jack does football fall quarter, and Brett goes to the After School Club with a bunch of the other second graders, so they won't get home for a while. Luckily, we're the only ones who take the 60 home, so as long as Jack and Brett have activities after school, I don't have to know anyone on the bus.

My back is completely sweating through my yellow T-shirt, and I sit on the edge of the shaded bench at the bus stop so my mammoth backpack can fit behind me. I always end up taking home books I don't need, but it's easier to get out of the building quickly if you just take everything. I squint in the sun. My mind wanders to the Resistance.

The Chicago street fades away, and I see a young girl, just my age. She's hiding alone on a dirty blanket in the dark, cold basement of the little house where I live with my mom and dad. When the world sleeps and it's safe, I knock gently on the basement door and bring her something to wear and what stale bread we can spare. She is thin and cold. Her deep, dark eyes meet mine as I loan her my gray, woolen dress.

"Hey, Grayson," a voice says softly, and I snap my head up. Amelia is standing next to the bench. Her dark eyes meet mine. "Do you take the 60?"

I jump up and accidentally knock my shoulder on her chest. Oh, God. "Sorry," I mumble. She looks down and takes a little step back. "Yeah. Um, do you?" I ask nervously.

Her cheeks are pink again. "Yeah, we live at the end of Randolph, right across from the lake."

"Really? What's your address?"

"One twenty-five Randolph," she says.

"I live right across the street from you," I tell her. You can see Amelia's building from our dining room window.

"Oh, cool. This is my first time riding the bus," she continues. "My mom drove me up till now. She said she'd drive me until I got used to things. So nice of her. Like that could make up for anything . . ." Her voice is sarcastic, and it trails off. She holds her red hair out of her face. The warm wind blows around us and becomes even hotter as the 60 pulls up at the stop.

I don't really know what to say, so I force myself to smile as I fish my bus pass out of my backpack pocket. Amelia unzips her messenger bag, takes out a tiny, hot-pink change purse, and finds her fresh, never-been-used pass. We climb the steps, and I walk to an empty seat. She wobbles over as the bus starts to move and sits down next to me. I look out the window and watch the cars and trucks pass by.

The bus ride is short and will be over soon. Out of the corner of my eye, I can see that Amelia is looking at me. I'm sure she wants to make new friends. I mean, nobody wants to be lonely—unless they *have* to be. Unless it's their only choice. So, I take a deep breath and turn to her. "What do you think of Porter?" I ask.

She seems relieved. "It's okay," she says. "I guess it's hard to tell. It seems pretty much like my old school, so far."

I nod. "Where'd you move from?"

"Boston," she says. "My mom got a promotion so we had to move here."

"Oh." I look down at Amelia's hands and try to think of what else to say. Her nails are all chewed up, like mine, and I can feel her body bumping and swaying next to me as the 60 makes its way over the potholed streets. We sit quietly for a couple of minutes, and I pretend to be interested in looking out the window.

"This is where we get off," I tell her when the bus finally slows down. Together, we stand up and walk to the doors. They open, then close behind us. We stand on the corner saying goodbye and see you tomorrow. She heads off down the street.

I cross the street slowly, watching my shoes as I go. Aside from talking about school stuff, that was probably the longest conversation I've had with anyone from Porter since second grade. When I get to the other side, I turn and watch Amelia's back as it disappears into the front door of her building before I walk the rest of the way home.

On the fifteenth floor, I unlock the door to our empty apartment. It's cool inside, and the air conditioning is humming away. I go to my bedroom, close the door, and stand in front of my mirror. My shoulders are sore from carrying my overstuffed, gray backpack, and I watch myself drop it by the foot of my bed.

My bangs cover my white sweatband, and my hair, which hangs just past my ears, has gotten all tangled up in the wind. I take the sweatband off, grab my brush from my desk, and comb through the knots. I put the sweatband back on so it pulls my bangs off my face, like a headband, but I know I can't keep it like that so I take it off altogether and throw it onto the bed as hard as I can. It lands silently. I study my sandy blond hair, thick and straight, and my blue eyes. I'm skinny enough that I seem lost in my shiny, bright yellow basketball pants and T-shirt, but my jaw doesn't look as pointed as it used to, and my shoulders seem more obvious underneath my shirt. I look down at my hands and think of Jack's hands and Uncle Evan's, and then I try to push these thoughts away.

I search the mirror for what I was able to see when I got dressed this morning—the long, shining, golden gown and the girl inside of it—but the image has completely vanished, just like I knew it would, because since sixth grade started, this has happened *every single day*. My imagination doesn't work like it used to. The basketball pants and T-shirt left in the gorgeous gown's place are pathetic.

I can practically hear the blood racing through my veins. Aunt Sally and Uncle Evan told me I used to have gigantic temper tantrums when I first moved here. I would rip the curtains off the windows, throw my desk chair across the room, and break everything I could. Everything, obviously, except for the old toys and pictures on my bookshelf. I'd never hurt those.

The urge to explode is rising in me now. I want to smash something into the mirror until I'm a million pieces on the ground, but I'm stuck in front of my reflection and I tell myself to breathe, to try harder.

I spin in a slow circle and my wide pants legs puff out like sails. I watch myself. They're still pants, and my chest tightens. I spin again, not like a dainty princess, but like a tornado. I'm making myself nauseous and dizzy, but I don't care. And finally, with the wave of a magic wand, with glitter flowing in its trail, in a blur of gold and a rush of hot blood and wind, my clothes transform, the way they have for so many years, into a dress.

I breathe deeply now. I know my pretend dress won't last for long, and tears sting my eyes. I sit at my desk and open the top drawer. The castle in my sketch is almost done, and I sharpen my gray colored pencil, lean over the sketch pad, and shade in the empty spaces. I draw the king and the queen outside in the garden, holding hands, and then, in the top window of the castle, so small that you can barely even see her, I draw the blond princess.

Suddenly, my bedroom door slams open and Jack barges in. I snap my sketch pad shut. I hadn't even heard anyone come home. "Dinner, loser," he announces.

I stand up in a fog. I am Cinderella. I follow my evil stepbrother to the dining room, wearing a golden gown that only I can see.

Chapter 3

THE WARM OCTOBER days fade into plain old November in Chicago. Some of the leaves still cling to the branches outside the tall, freshly cleaned windows at Porter. They're fiery orange, red, and yellow against the gray-white sky. They're like flames dangling from the trees—like something you'd see in a painting.

I'm sitting at my desk, doodling in the margins of my notebook. "We're starting a new novel today," Finn is saying, and I look up to watch him excitedly carry a stack of books to his desk from the bookshelf.

"Are we going to have to write a paper on it?" Lila calls out. She glances around the room, probably to make sure that everyone's watching her. And for the most part, everyone is.

"Great question, Lila, thank you!" Finn says, smiling. "We are!"

Practically the whole class groans.

Meagan, who sits right in front of me, tucks her thin, black hair behind her ears and fixes her eyes on Lila, who is still glancing around the room. Meagan looks interested, but also sort of annoyed. She and Lila have been friends forever. All of a sudden, I wonder what she thinks of her.

"We'll have lots to discuss as we read," Finn continues. "Starting today, all of my classes will be working in pairs for the rest of the quarter. You're the lucky ones who get to rearrange the classroom. Once you're paired up, everyone will have a built-in discussion partner!"

I look up quickly, then down, as my hands get clammy. "So," Finn continues, "everybody up! Find your partners! Once you've pushed your desks together into pairs, I want the pairs lined up in rows!" He's yelling now over the noise of the class. It's like someone broke a piñata, and everyone is frantically searching for candy. Except for me. I stand up slowly, and I don't move. *It's not such a big deal!* I want to scream. But I'm frozen.

I've done this so many times before. Teachers at Porter are always making us choose partners for projects, or choose groups for discussions. By now, I've figured out what to do. I stand still. I watch kids pair up frantically. They look so stupid. I wait. In the end, the teacher will suggest that I join up with Keri or Michael or whoever is left over.

Across the room, Ryan motions for Sebastian to join him, and

Hailey and Lila are already laughing about something as they push their desks together. Amelia is in the middle of the room, looking around nervously. She always sits next to me on the bus now. I'm starting to feel jittery. She says something to Maria and then looks down, her face flushed. She glances around again. It almost looks like she's about to cry.

She starts walking in my direction. Now my heart is racing in my chest. *Nothing* is working for me the way it used to, and all the sounds around me start to disappear, like someone is turning the volume button on the radio almost to off. The only noise I can hear is an annoying hum, and suddenly, it's like I'm watching myself watch the class, as if I'm a bird perched on the high wooden bookshelves lining the classroom walls. I see myself below, biting my lip, clumsily untying the oversize gray sweatshirt from my waist. I watch myself look down and retie it, trying to stretch it so it hangs around my waist completely. I see myself study the small gap in front. The sweatshirt isn't big enough to be a skirt. And, then, from my perch up above, I start to feel like someone's watching *me*, like I'm a bird in a cage. I look over to Finn. He's sitting on his desk, his head cocked to the side. He looks at the sweatshirt around my waist and back up to my eyes.

With a thump, I'm back on the ground. Amelia is standing in front of me. The volume has been switched back on. Desks and chairs scream across the floor.

She looks nervous. "So, do *you* already have a partner, too?" she asks.

"No," I mumble.

"Do you want to pair up, then?" she asks quickly.

I can't think of a reason to say no, so I nod. "Yeah, okay." We push our desks together at the back of the room behind Ryan and Sebastian, and sit down. Finn is dancing around the classroom directing pairs to move six inches this way or that. I smooth out my hair and look down at my nails. I can feel Amelia's eyes on me.

"So, I never see you at lunch," she says. Her voice is loud over the sounds of the classroom, and I cringe. She continues, "Do you have a different lunch period or something?"

In front of us, Ryan and Sebastian grin at each other and turn around. Sebastian adjusts his glasses. "He's eaten lunch in the library since, like, third grade," he says.

I try not to flinch, and I look at Amelia. She's blushing. "Oh," she says quietly.

"I bet he's doing extra homework," Ryan says, smirking. "Like the teachers don't already love him. What a freak." I look back down at my fingernails.

Finn is back in the front of the newly arranged classroom, yelling for our attention. Ryan and Sebastian turn around, and I look up at Amelia out of the corner of my eye. Her cheeks look pink, and she's staring straight ahead.

"We only have a minute left," Finn says once the class is quiet. "Here are your books. Please read chapters one through three tonight." He hands out stacks of novels quickly at the front of the room, counting out the right numbers for each row.

Sebastian passes two books back to me without turning around. I hand one to Amelia, and she puts it into her backpack. I do the same.

The bell rings. Once Ryan and Sebastian are out of earshot, Amelia turns to me. Almost whispering, she says, "I think you should meet me in the lunchroom fifth period. We could eat together."

I think, suddenly, of second grade, before Emma moved away, and of the table in the corner of the lunchroom where we always used to sit. I look at Amelia's round face and dimpled cheeks.

I feel myself stepping out of my skin again. "Okay," I say. I have no control over myself. "I'll meet you there."

Chapter 4

I HAVEN'T SET FOOT in the lunchroom in forever. It's crazy how loud it is. I guess the entire middle school is jammed into one room, so what did I expect? Everyone is crammed in, close together, leaning over tables, throwing brown paper bags, getting up, sitting down, yelling, laughing. The smell of hot lunches and old sandwiches is so disgusting that it's almost unbearable. I look over to where a bunch of seventh graders are sitting, and I scan their faces quickly for Jack, but luckily, I don't see him anywhere.

The ceiling of the lunchroom is high, and long rectangular windows line three sides of the room completely. A flood of blinding light pours in from outside. The noise bounces like a million invisible Ping-Pong balls from the floor to the ceiling to the windows to the tops of the lunch tables over and over again.

I stand in the doorway, feeling completely ill. I wonder where Jack is. The strap of my backpack is cutting into my shoulder, and I can't take it anymore. I turn around to head to the library. But I take one step and walk right into Amelia.

"Good, you came!" she says. "Come on." She steps ahead of me, into the lunchroom. I take one more look around, and I follow her in.

She walks slowly down the aisle in the center of the room, looking carefully at each table she passes until she finally stops when she gets to a pretty empty one near the back of the room. Lila, Meagan, Hannah, and Hailey are sitting toward the middle of the long table, huddled together in a little clump, their lunch bags in front of them and their lunches spread out on the tabletop. "Let's sit here," Amelia says quickly, and she plops her backpack down on the end of the table. "Are you buying lunch?"

I slide onto the bench and unzip my backpack. "No, I brought one." I take out the brown bag that Aunt Sally packed last night.

"Yeah, me too," Amelia says, taking a pink lunch bag out of her backpack. "You couldn't pay me to eat hot lunch." She glances over to the four girls and looks quickly back to me. I peer over at them to see what she's looking at, but they're just sitting there, eating and talking.

"I know," I tell her, and smile a little. I watch her unwrap her sandwich. She takes a bite, and I wonder who she ate with before today. Probably nobody.

My stomach is fluttery and empty feeling. Up through second grade, Emma and I used to eat lunch together every day. Across the room, some eighth-grade boys are sitting at the table near the glass doors where we always used to eat. Looking between them to the empty playground outside makes me think of friendship bracelets made out of colorful yarn and the way Emma would tuck her shirt into her jeans before we'd hang upside down on the jungle gym. I smile to myself thinking about her messy blond hair, red-rimmed glasses, and missing front teeth.

It doesn't feel like I'm supposed to be here, in this loud, crowded room filled with shouting and laughing, but a part of me—the part of me that also wonders how Emma's doing in Florida, if that's even where she still lives—is happy to be back.

I bite into my sandwich, chew slowly, and wonder what to say to Amelia. She's glancing around. Her eyes jump from one group of sixth graders to another. She looks again at Lila, Meagan, Hannah, and Hailey, and smiles this time. When I look over, I see that Lila is waving to her.

Amelia turns back to me, beaming, and takes another bite of her sandwich. "So, it's cool that Finn lets us pick our own groups," she says, her mouth full. "We never got to do anything like that at my old school."

"Yeah," I say, as I dig through my lunch bag for my water bottle. "We always get to do that kind of thing."

"That's awesome," she says, opening her pretzels.

She starts telling me about Boston, and I wonder if she had lots of friends at her old school. It's like I stepped inside a bubble with Amelia. The bright light, noises, and smells bounce off of it.

Amelia is still talking when the lunch monitor gets to our table and tells us to line up at the glass doors for sixth period. It's strange to think that life in the lunchroom went on without me during all the years I was eating by myself in the library. I wonder for another second if I'm making a mistake, but I smile at Amelia anyway, stuff the rest of my lunch into my backpack, and follow her to the double doors.

After school, I watch for Amelia at the bus stop. She shows up a few minutes after me, and we get on the 60 together. We always sit in the same seats now.

"So, what do you do after school?" I blurt out, and immediately look out the window. I don't want to see her reaction.

She doesn't seem fazed. "Nothing. Watch TV, homework. My mom comes home at, like, six, and we have dinner." I picture Amelia alone in her fancy marble apartment, and I feel sorry for her. It seems lonely, and I look at her eyes to see if I can find the sadness.

"Where does your dad live?" I ask.

"Just outside of Boston. I used to go to his house every weekend, but now that we moved I'm going for the summers instead." She says it as if she's telling me about a math assignment, like it's no big deal.

"Do you like him?" I ask.

"He's nice when it's just me and him, but I can't stand his wife and I have two prissy little stepsisters who everyone thinks are perfect." She's talking fast now. "They're five and seven, and they're such brats. And his wife is so whiney and obnoxious. I can't stand them." She spits the last sentence out like it's a piece of old, disgusting gum.

"Oh." I look at her. Her body bounces as the bus bumps along. Her jeans are kind of frumpy, and her arms are folded over her dark pink fleece, like she's trying to hide herself. I envision two perfect little girls in perfect matching outfits, and I am positive that Amelia feels like an outcast. I understand how she feels, and I look out the window again and squeeze my eyes shut.

I think back to all the other kids in the lunchroom, sitting together in clumps, huddled around their own shared secrets. I take a deep breath and turn back to Amelia. "So, do you want to go shopping with me this weekend? There's this great thrift shop in Lake View that I've been wanting to go to."

She looks at me for a second, her head tilted to the side. She seems curious and surprised. "Really?"

"Yeah!" I say. I'm excited, but I catch myself. "Our old nanny used to take us all the time, but I haven't been in forever. I need winter clothes." The bus is slowing to a stop. We stand up, make our way to the door, and jump down. "My aunt and uncle usually just give me money and let me shop by myself. They don't really care what I do." I'm surprised that I say this; I'm not really sure if it's true.

She pauses again and watches my eyes as the bus disappears down the street. She pulls her hair away from her face. "You live with your aunt and uncle?"

"Yeah," I say, jamming my hands into my pockets. I look down the street, away from Amelia. "Listen, I have to get home. Ask your mom if you can come with me. Tomorrow or Sunday. It doesn't matter. Call me. You have the school directory, right?"

"Yeah," she says, still studying me as I turn quickly to cross the street. I run across as the bright hand starts to blink. My giant backpack suddenly feels like two hands collapsing my shoulders. It thuds against my back as I run. The wind has picked up off the lake at the end of the block, and it wails through the tall buildings like the siren on an ambulance. I turn around when I get to the corner and look back at Amelia through my long, windblown bangs. She's still standing where I left her. She raises her hand slowly and gives me a little wave. I smile quickly, then turn and walk home.

Chapter 5

I LET MYSELF into the empty apartment and go straight to my room. I throw my backpack onto my bed as I watch my reflection in the mirror out of the corner of my eye. My black jeans are jeans. My oversize, long-sleeved T-shirt is a T-shirt. The girl in the leggings and dress who I struggled to see this morning was gone by the time I'd finished breakfast. I slam my bedroom door and walk to the kitchen for some cereal. *You're getting way too old to pretend,* I tell myself.

I shove what I wish I saw in the mirror out of my mind and think back, instead, to my conversation with Amelia. I wonder if she'll call me. Maybe I'll have a real friend again. I think, for the first time in forever, of Emma's apartment and how her mom would give us lunch on the kid-size wooden table in her living room. I remember pink plastic bowls of macaroni and cheese, and juice boxes. My body feels strange, like it's someone else's, and I shudder, because I could be making a huge mistake.

I bring my cereal to my room, avoiding the mirror this time. Instead, I pull out my sketch pad and colored pencils, and focus on the field of flowers that I'm working on. I draw the flowers on their stems—each one different from the one next to it. I think about adding two girls in the middle of the field, but I hear the front door click open and Jack and Brett talking, so I slide the drawing into my drawer, take my math book out of my backpack, and start my homework instead. I glance at the clock. Aunt Sally and Uncle Evan will be home soon, too.

There's a knock on my door, and Brett pokes his head in. "Hi, Grayson," he says through the crack. "Whatcha doing? I need to show you something."

"Cool, what is it?" I ask, putting down my pencil. He walks over to me until our noses are practically touching, and he opens his mouth. "You guess," he says as best he can with his mouth open wide. "What's different?"

I peer inside. "Looks like there's a tooth missing," I say. He grins and pulls a tiny red plastic treasure chest out from his pocket. He pries it open to show me. I remember getting the same thing from the nurse's office at school when I was younger. "That's awesome," I tell him even though the tooth looks gross. "Don't lose it."

He snaps the treasure chest shut. "I won't." He shoves it back into his pocket and walks over to my bookcase. "Can I?" he asks. I nod. He picks up my old brown teddy bear and the small greenish one, and jumps onto my bed with them.

"What's Jack doing?" I ask him, and he shrugs as he adjusts the T-shirt on the brown bear. Probably lying on the couch with his eyes closed, listening to music again.

I do my math problems while Brett plays on my bed. Eventually, I hear the front door open and close, and then dinnertime noises. Uncle Evan is talking to Jack. "Don't you have homework?" he's asking, and Aunt Sally is saying something about setting the table.

Brett puts the bears back onto the shelf carefully, right next to my old picture books, and we walk to the dining room. White boxes of Chinese takeout are scattered on the gleaming glass table. Uncle Evan asks us how school was and did we do our homework—the same questions every day. I sit next to Brett and start opening containers as he shows Aunt Sally, Uncle Evan, and Jack his treasure chest and the hole in his mouth.

"Make sure you put that tooth under the pillow for the tooth fairy," Uncle Evan reminds Brett as Jack rolls his eyes.

"Jack," Aunt Sally warns, shooting him a look. "So," she says, "aside from Brett finally losing his tooth, did anything exciting happen today?" She pauses, looking at us expectantly, but no one answers. Her eyes look tired. "Hey, Ev," she says like she just remembered something, "my prediction about Felix and that brief was absolutely right on. Can you believe that?"

"I can," Uncle Evan responds. "So, what happened?"

And they go on, discussing some legal situation while Brett shows me how he can poke his straw into the new window in the side of his mouth and drink his milk through it. Eventually, he almost spills, and Uncle Evan makes him stop. I stare out the floor-to-ceiling windows at Amelia's building and the darkening sky.

Aunt Sally is stacking our plates into a pile when the phone rings. Jack jumps up and darts into the kitchen.

"Hello?" he asks. There's a pause, and he comes around the corner into the dining room with the phone to his ear. He has a giant, annoying grin plastered on his stupid face. "Who's calling?" he asks, his eyes sparkling. "One moment please," he sings, in a phony, polite voice.

He keeps the phone next to his face. "Um, Grayson, it seems your girlfriend, Amelia, is calling?"

I jump up. "Shut up, Jack," I say. I hold out my hand for the phone. He isn't budging. I look at Aunt Sally and Uncle Evan for help, but they're just looking back and forth between me and Jack, shocked.

"Jack, is it really for Grayson?" Uncle Evan finally asks.

Jack grins. "I'm serious; it is!"

"So why aren't you giving it to him?" Brett asks, and Uncle Evan startles.

"Yes, Jack, just hand him the phone," Uncle Evan says, glancing over at Aunt Sally, who now has a pleased smile on her face.

Jack extends his arm slowly, and I snatch the phone from his hand. I walk to my room and sit on the edge of my bed.

"Hello?" I almost whisper.

"Hi, it's me, Amelia," she says. "Who was that?"

"Just my cousin Jack. Ignore him. He's a complete jerk."

"Yeah, seriously," Amelia says. "How old is he? Does he go to Porter? Did you tell him I'm not your girlfriend?"

"What?" I ask.

"He called me your girlfriend. Did you tell him I wasn't?"

"Oh—no, I will," I say.

"Okay." She pauses. "Grayson?"

"Yeah?" I realize I'm holding the phone to my ear with both hands.

"So, I'm free tomorrow. What time do you want to go?"

"You can go?"

"Yeah, but my mom wants to know what time the bus leaves and where exactly we're going."

I smile. "Okay! Great! We can leave whenever you want. The express buses run all the time on the weekends. It's in Lake View, on the corner of Broadway and Belmont. I don't know the exact address, but I can find out. It's called the Second Hand. Want me to look it up?"

"No, that's okay. I'll tell her. Do you want to meet at the bus stop at ten?"

"Yeah, that's perfect!" I say.

"Okay, see you tomorrow."

"Great. Bye."

I end the call and sit back down on my bed for a minute, beaming. I stay that way until I feel up to explaining to Aunt Sally and Uncle Evan that I have plans with a friend for the first time since second grade.

Chapter 6

I ZIP MY dark purple sweatshirt to my chin and put up the hood to block out the Chicago wind as I head for the bus stop. I glance down at my wide, gray, shiny track pants. The foggy image of the skirt that I saw in the mirror this morning is already flickering and fading. I think I can feel Aunt Sally, Uncle Evan, Jack, and Brett watching me from the living room window fifteen floors up, but I don't turn around to check.

Amelia is making her way down the street, and I try to forget that my pants are still pants as I wave to her and smile. Her chin is buried in the neck of a red peacoat. I really should have worn something warmer. It's freezing out.

"Hi!" I say as she joins me under the glass enclosure. Her eyes look pink. "Do you have a cold or something?" Then I realize that she's been crying, and I feel like an idiot. She takes a crumpled, used-looking piece of tissue out of her pocket and blows her nose.

She takes a deep breath. "Sometimes I just hate my mom," she says, blowing her nose again. She shoves the tissue and her hands into her pockets.

"Oh," I say. It's like the words are nothing to her. *My mom.* I look at her blotchy face, and for a second, I try to imagine what it would be like to be able to hate your mom, but I don't even want to think about it. "Why?" I finally force myself to ask.

"She's just constantly hounding me about the way I look. She was so excited when I told her I was going shopping. She was like, 'Be sure to get some tops to flatter your figure.' She may as well just tell me I'm fat and ugly." She sits down on the bench and slouches forward.

"That's ridiculous," I tell her. "That's so obnoxious." I search for the right words, but I don't know exactly what to say.

"Whatever," she says. "It doesn't matter. I'm used to it."

The bus pulls up. We sit in the back. She takes a deep breath and pushes her hair out of her face.

"So, why do you live with your aunt and uncle?" she asks as the bus starts to move.

I feel like I've been hit from behind by a wave of lava, and even though I'm still freezing, I'm suddenly sweating. I'm an idiot for not knowing the question was coming, for not rehearsing. I know I can't avoid answering. *This is what having friends means,* I tell myself.

I haven't had to talk about it for so long—not since Aunt Sally and Uncle Evan made me do those sessions with that stupid therapist in fourth grade. I think about his office and the paintings and drawings on the walls that other kids made for him in his "art studio." What losers, I remember thinking. What pushovers. What could this guy possibly be doing for them that's so great? The thought made me furious then, and it makes me furious now. *You need to stop isolating yourself at school,* he used to tell me. He didn't know anything about me.

But maybe Amelia could. She's studying me. I have to say something, so I take a deep breath, stare at the seat in front of me, and start to talk.

"When I was four, my parents died," I tell her. I talk fast. "We lived in Cleveland. There was a car accident. It was really bad. It was on the highway. There was this truck that swerved into their lane, and they were killed instantly." I glance at her quickly. She's staring at me, and I look down at my feet, at my dark blue gym shoes that are almost purple. "I was at preschool when it happened."

I feel like I'm reading from a storybook, and I want to slam it closed now and throw it out the window like it's on fire. I look at Lake Michigan. The waves are white and wild next to the gray highway. Two trucks fly past us. I realize I'm not breathing, and I force myself to.

"Oh," Amelia says quietly.

I stare at the dust and dirt that's shoved into the crevice around the metal window frame next to me, and for some reason,

I think of my old blue house. I don't remember it, but I have a picture of it on the bookshelf in my room. There's a FOR SALE sign on the front lawn with one of those SOLD banners crossing over it. Uncle Evan told me that he tried to get the real estate lady to take the sign down for the picture, but she said it was too much trouble. I don't know why, but I wonder about the people who bought it. I wonder if they painted it, or if the house is still blue.

"It was bad," I say. "But I don't remember it at all. My uncle Evan is my dad's brother, so I came to live with them."

"Oh my God," she says, and then she's quiet again. It seems like I should say something else.

"My grandma Alice lives here, too. She's really sick now. Anyway, I guess it made sense for me to come to Chicago."

"Oh my God," she says again, and I don't know what else to say.

For a while, both of us are quiet. I watch out the window as the bus pulls off the highway. "So have you been to Lake View?" I finally ask her as we slow down at the bus stop, thankful to have something else to talk about.

"What? No," she says, as she follows me off the bus. We stand at the corner in a crowd of people. "Maybe I should consider myself lucky," she says as we cross the street. She stares straight ahead as she talks. Her long, red hair is blowing across her cheek.

"I guess so," I say.

"I mean, maybe I don't have it as bad as I thought."

I look at her round, solid face, and I open the door of the

Second Hand. She walks in, up the sloped wooden floor that looks like it has survived a thousand floods, between the circular racks of clothes, and toward the YOUTH sign that hangs crookedly at the back of the store. I follow her.

A guy behind the counter with a shaved head, earrings, and a nose ring says hey to me as I pass him. Two women dressed in black layers and wearing bright lipstick sift through the clothes on a rack.

We're the only ones in the back of the store. There are fewer racks of clothes back here, and the back door is cracked open so the air isn't quite as thick with the scent of mothballs, which is good because the smell makes me want to vomit. To the side are three minuscule dressing rooms with old bedsheets for doors and a giant mirror is propped against the wall. I stand in front of it and study my skinny body. My purple hood is still up and I take it down, unzip my sweatshirt, and run my fingers through my hair. I push my bangs carefully to the side of my forehead. My eyes sting from the cold air outside, my nose is pink, and I notice again how my chin looks squarer and less pointed than it used to.

Uncle Evan has shown me pictures of Dad when he was my age, and I know I look like him. The thought makes me want to smash the mirror. I shove my fists into my pockets because what I *really* want is for Dad to be here, and I wonder for the millionth time if I'd still have to be this lonely if Mom and Dad were alive. In old black-and-white pictures, Grandma Alice looks just like

Mom did. I search my face in the mirror for any hint of her or Mom in me, but I can only see Dad.

I quickly walk to where Amelia is browsing in the girls' section. Her coat is in a neat pile on the floor near one of the dressing room doors, and she's searching through a rack labeled GIRLS' DRESSES AND SKIRTS in messy writing on a laminated sign. "What do you think of this one?" she asks, pulling out a deep purple, floor-length skirt. The fabric is thin and scrunched, like an accordion, and is interrupted three times by bands of deep purple lace. The lace pulls the fabric in and makes soft swells. I stare at it.

"It's great," I say, and I reach out to touch the fabric.

"Are you looking for anything?" Amelia asks. She quickly drapes the skirt over her arm. "I thought you needed winter clothes."

"Oh, yeah," I say, and walk to the boys' racks, still watching her out of the corner of my eye. I filter through the hangers, but really I pay attention to Amelia on the other side of the room. She's collecting a pile of clothes—deep pinks and purples, laces and embroidered flowers, and they're draped over her arm like shimmery gowns from a fairy tale.

The clothes I run my fingers over are way less majestic. I search halfheartedly for shirts that are narrow but extra long, colorful plaids, and bright fabrics. I pull out a green, metallic-looking Green Bay Packers jersey. The sleeves glisten in the artificial light, and I walk to the mirror with it and hold it in front of my chest. It's too long, and would come down almost to my knees. I could ignore the lettering on it. With my old jeans that are too tight now, I could imagine it's a sparkling dress over leggings.

"What'd you find?" Amelia asks, walking over to me with her soft pile of clothing still hanging tenderly over her arm.

I study the image of the football jersey in the mirror. *Green Bay Packers* screams at me from the chest. "Ah, nothing," I say, and hang it on the rack closest to me. "It's too big." My imagination is failing me. I'm way too old to play dress-up. I look down at my feet. My purplish blue shoes look completely blue in the bright lights.

"Are you sure?" Amelia asks. "Do you want to try it on? I'm going to try these on."

"Nah," I say, taking a deep breath. "It's okay. It's hit or miss in secondhand shops. They don't have much in my size this time."

"Okay," she says, walking away. She lets herself into a dressing room, and I sit on a stiff, metal chair next to the mirrors where I don't have to look at myself. I study the scratches on the wood floor. Amelia comes out to examine how she looks in each new dress, skirt, and top. She stares at herself for a long time in the purple skirt. "I don't know," she says, cocking her head to the side. "Do people at Porter wear things like this?"

I sit up straight and look at her carefully. "I mean, not all the time," I tell her. "But I think it's fantastic."

In the end, she puts it back on the rack. She buys a shorter black skirt with a flouncy ribbon around the bottom and a white T-shirt with flowers embroidered around the neck. I am empty-handed as we leave the store. I didn't realize it had started to rain while we were inside. I pull up my hood against the drizzle, and we board the bus for home.

Chapter 7

AMELIA AND I go to the Second Hand every Saturday in November. She tries on clothes and sometimes finds something to buy. Unexcitedly, I search the boys' racks. One windy morning, I give up on the idea of finding anything I'll like. I leave Amelia behind and walk away from the boys' section to the shelves of knickknacks at the front of the store.

"Who buys this stuff?" Amelia asks, suddenly by my side.

"Are you done shopping?"

"Yeah, they don't have anything good today." Amelia runs her hands over dusty vases and grimy statues of sleeping cats and prancing horses.

"Hey, look at this!" I pick up an old golden birdcage with a blue plastic bird on a perch inside. I turn it around in my hands. On the side is the thing to wind it with.

I twist the knob and put it back on the shelf. Amelia and I stand there. For a minute nothing happens, but then the bird slowly starts to flap its dusty, feathered wings, like it's finally waking up from a super-long nap. Old-fashioned, rusty-sounding music chimes. The notes are creaky and uneven, and the fluttering becomes jerkier as Amelia and I watch. It looks like the bird is trying to fly through glue, but its wings keep getting stuck. We glance at each other, and Amelia starts to giggle.

Suddenly, the bird freezes, its wings outstretched, and, in slow motion, it tips over and falls off its metal perch. Amelia grabs my arm. "Oh my God, I think we broke it," she whispers, fixing her mouth into a frown, trying hard not to laugh. The bird is lying on the floor of the cage, one of its wings still twitching, as the music continues to ping. It almost looks like the bird is trying to get up and fly away.

It's kind of depressing to see it lying there like that, but I smile at Amelia anyway. "Let's get out of here!" she whispers, laughing. I look behind me. The man at the register is staring at us. Amelia is hysterical now, and I quickly drag her outside. I can hear the still-dying chirps of tinny music until the door clicks shut behind us.

Outside, the cold air is sharp. Amelia collapses in laughter on the concrete steps of the Second Hand, and I sit down next to her. I guess it's stupid to feel bad for a plastic bird, and watching

Amelia laugh so hard makes me start to laugh, too. "We totally broke it," she finally says, trying to compose herself.

"Come on," I say, standing up, still laughing. "It's freezing. Want to get hot chocolate? There's a coffee shop down the street." I grab her hands and pull her up.

When we get to the coffee shop, she saves us two seats at the bar by the window while I order our hot chocolates and a marshmallow square to share. We hold the paper cups in our freezing hands. Our reflections are pale and blotchy in the giant window. The people walking on the sidewalk pass through them. They're so close that we could touch them if the wall of glass wasn't there.

Amelia takes the lid off of her paper cup and dunks a piece of marshmallow square in. I watch her and do the same thing. "Next Saturday, I'll take you to this other coffee shop a few blocks that way," I tell her, pointing out the window. "Our nanny used to take us all the time. They have way better snacks."

"Cool," she says, as she swivels back and forth on her stool and smiles.

Back home, Aunt Sally looks up from her laptop when I let myself into the front door. "Grayson," she says, lifting her reading glasses onto her head. She puts the laptop next to her. "How was your morning with Amelia?"

"It was great," I say.

"I'm so glad." Aunt Sally smiles at me and then looks down at her fingernails for a second.

"Grayson, honey?" she says, looking back up, her face serious now. "Your uncle Evan is planning to go over to the nursing home. He got a call from Adele when you were out. Your grandma . . ." She pauses and tilts her head softly to the side. My heart jumps. "Well, you know she's been more and more confused, lately. And Adele said she took a nap this morning and when she woke up, she had a fever. The doctors are worried that she might have pneumonia."

"Oh," I say, and I feel sort of guilty because I should be thinking of Grandma Alice, sick in her bed at the nursing home, but I'm not. She's had Alzheimer's for practically as long as I can remember. I'm thinking instead of the black-and-white picture on my nightstand of me, Mom, and Dad. You can only see our faces, but you can tell that Mom was tickling me. My back is smushed into her, and I'm laughing. Dad's arm is around us both.

"'Kay," I say. I know I sound nervous, and I can tell Aunt Sally is waiting for me to say more, but my brain feels stuck. I don't feel like standing there anymore, and I head for my room.

A few minutes later, Uncle Evan quietly taps on my door. He lets himself in and sits on my bed. I'm standing in front of the mirror tying my hooded sweatshirt around my waist. I'm trying to see it as a purple skirt, but I can't focus. I keep thinking again of how in all the pictures I have of Mom, she looks like a young version of Grandma Alice.

"Grayson?" Uncle Evan starts.

"Yeah?"

"Why don't you come with me to the home to see your grandma?" I give up on the sweatshirt and throw it onto my bed. It lands on my pillow next to the picture on my nightstand. Uncle Evan and Aunt Sally aren't even related to Grandma Alice. They wouldn't be taking care of her if it weren't for me.

"Okay," I say.

"Good. Do you think you can be ready in fifteen minutes or so?" he asks. I nod, and he drums his fingers on his knees as I sit down at my desk chair. I pull my colored pencils and sketch pad out of the top drawer and stare at my half-finished drawing of a rose bush. I hate the nursing home. It's so depressing.

"So, Grayson," Uncle Evan finally says, "Aunt Sally and I were talking last night. We want you to know how glad we are that you've made a new friend. You seem happier now that you're hanging around with Amelia, and we think it's really fantastic." He smiles. "Did I ever tell you that your Aunt Sally and I met when we were in sixth grade?"

"Really?" I ask, but then I look down quickly. I know what he's getting at. "It's not like that," I tell him. "We're just friends."

"Of course," he stammers. "I didn't mean . . ."

"It's okay," I tell him, and I smile to try to make him feel better. In pictures of Mom, you can see that she had the same wrinkles on the sides of her eyes that Grandma Alice has. Once, a long, long time ago, Grandma Alice told me they were matching smile wrinkles. I reach up and touch the side of my face, but it's smooth.

"Well, okay, then," Uncle Evan says, getting up off my bed. He stops behind me on his way to the door and pauses, placing his hand on my shoulder as I pick up a red colored pencil.

"Really, son, we're glad you're happier." I cringe. He gives my shoulder a little squeeze. "I'll let you know when I'm ready." He shuts the door quietly and completely behind him.

Even though the nursing home is supposedly a nice one, it's gross, and it smells like rubbing alcohol, Band-Aids, and old people. In the elevator there's a nurse and an old man with a walker. I try not to stare at him. He's trying to talk, but no words are coming out. It's like he's chewing on air, and my eyes sting.

We walk down the long hallway to Grandma Alice's room. Inside, everything is the same as it has always been, only this time instead of sitting in the rocking chair next to the window, smoothing out the blanket on her lap over and over again, Grandma Alice is in her bed. The back is propped up, and someone attached the metal rails to the sides. Her eyes are open but I can tell that she's not looking at anything.

Uncle Evan and I stand next to her for a minute. "Hi, Grandma," I say, but she doesn't answer and Uncle Evan puts his hand on my shoulder again. Adele reaches over and gently picks up Grandma Alice's arm so she can wrap the blood pressure cuff around it. She takes her blood pressure, writes something on a clipboard, and then she and Uncle Evan start to talk.

I wander around the room. "She still hasn't eaten. . . ." I hear Adele start to say. I try to ignore them, but it's hard to in such a small room.

I look at the pictures on Grandma Alice's dresser. They're kind of dusty and I wipe them off on my shirt one by one as Adele keeps talking to Uncle Evan in a hushed voice. "Her symptoms definitely point to pneumonia," she's saying. Grandma Alice has the same photo as I do of our blue house in Cleveland. Mom and Dad met in Chicago and moved to Cleveland just before I was born so Mom could take a job teaching at the university. I wonder again what my life would be like if she hadn't gotten that job and they'd stayed in Chicago. And I wonder again about the house, if it's still blue.

I pick up a picture of me with Grandpa Lefty. He died when I was two. I'm sitting on his lap on the front porch of their old house in just a diaper. There's a black-and-white picture of Grandma Alice when she was a baby with dimpled cheeks, short bangs, and a round belly, and one of Grandma Alice and Grandpa Lefty on their wedding day.

Then I pick up my favorites: Mom riding a bike when she was about my age, her eyes squinting in the sun and a shirt tied around her waist, floating behind her in the breeze; Mom and Dad kissing in front of their wedding cake; and the one of me as a baby, mostly hidden under a blanket, lying on Mom's chest.

"I don't think it will be long now, but you know Alice—she's a fighter," Adele says as I drift back over to them. Grandma Alice is sitting in the same position, but now her eyes are closed, and she's breathing deeply and kind of raggedly.

"Well," Uncle Evan says. Gently, he straightens the blanket on Grandma Alice's lap and doesn't say anything else. A clump of her white hair has fallen over her face, and I braid it loosely and tuck it behind her ear so it won't unravel. I can feel Uncle Evan watching me as I pick up her soft, bumpy, paper-thin hand. The skin droops between the bones, like a row of tiny bridges. Mom grew inside of her, I think to myself, and I replay the feel of her skin on my hand the whole way home.

Chapter 8

IT'S DREARY on Monday morning. Finn is standing in front of the windows, trying to start a discussion as gentle snow swirls outside behind him. I watch him, my chin resting in my hands. Amelia is doodling lazily on the cover of her notebook next to me, and I'm thinking of Grandma Alice's room—of the dusty pictures and the hospital bed. And of what Adele said.

Finn keeps asking the class questions, but nobody's talking. "Okay," he finally sighs, "enough of this! You obviously don't want to talk to me. Everybody, stay with your partner and pair up with another group to make a foursome. You guys can discuss the passages from the book in small groups. Remember, next Monday I'll be assigning your big papers, so stay focused!"

Everybody, including Amelia, starts looking around nervously.

"Go ahead," Finn says, hoisting himself up onto the window ledge, looking amused. "Let the mad dash for partners commence!"

I pick up my book and backpack, and follow Amelia's lead. Her eyes are fixed on Lila and Hailey across the room, and she walks quickly over to them. I feel like a dog on a leash following her.

"Hey, guys," she says, approaching them. "Can we join you?"

Lila glances across the room to where Meagan and Hannah are already sitting with two other girls, their backs to us. "Sure," she says, after a second.

"Pull up Jason's and Asher's chairs," Hailey adds, smiling. We sit down, and I turn my chair so I don't have to look at Ryan and Sebastian, who are at the desks right next to us.

"So, what do you guys think of these passages?" Lila asks, looking at the three of us. Of course she wants us to do all the work.

"I thought the second one Finn was talking about was the most interesting," Hailey says, flipping back in her book to find it.

I watch her as she searches through the pages. The summer before third grade, I did art camp with her and Hannah. I remember stringing beads onto pieces of elastic with them at the playground. By then, Emma was already gone. I suddenly wonder why I didn't stay friends with them once third grade started; I suddenly wonder why Emma was the *only* one.

"Here it is!" Hailey says. "Page fifty." I flip to it in my book. She starts to read but I barely listen.

At art camp, sometimes we'd go to the park with our little easels and paints. I remember kids making paintings of the swing set, the giant trees, and the flowers and vegetables that some other camp groups had planted. This one time Hannah and Hailey and I were painting together at the edge of the garden. I was trying to make a gigantic orange tiger lily with watercolors, but both of them just wanted to paint these little sprouts that were poking through the dirt.

I look at the tiny freckles on Hailey's nose as she finishes the passage. When she's done, she takes off her turquoise headband and runs her fingers through her light brown hair. Then she puts it back in, making tiny, delicate comb marks, collecting the wisps.

I touch my sweatband on my forehead and take it off as Amelia starts writing down notes in big, loopy handwriting. I turn the sweatband around in my hands. It's grayish-white with sweat stains. I try to imagine it's turquoise, but it's still grayish-white and disgusting.

I think back to fifth grade when all I had to do was *pretend* and everything would be okay.

Outside the window, the powdering of snow is still making its way down to the ground, and Finn is still perched on the window ledge. His eyes wander to the sweatband in my hand. He smiles gently when our eyes meet. I look away and put it back on. Finally, he hops down and makes his way around the classroom to listen in on everyone's discussions. When the bell rings, we pack up our stuff. "So," Lila says, looking mostly at Amelia, "you should sit with us at lunch." She stands up and straightens her pink shirt under her backpack straps.

I look to Amelia quickly. "Okay, great!" she says, smiling up at Lila.

I swallow hard and Lila looks at me. "You, too, Grayson," she adds. "If you want."

I look from her to Amelia, nod and smile. "Okay," I say.

"Great," Amelia adds, beaming. "We'll see you fifth period."

At lunchtime, Amelia and I sit with the girls in the middle of the table. We spread our lunches out in front of us. The tabletop is crowded with water bottles and half-filled plastic bags. Hannah takes a rubber band off her wrist and gathers her curly brown hair into a ponytail. She glances at me for a second and smiles. I wonder if she still paints, and I almost ask her, but I don't. Amelia rests her elbows on the table next to me as she talks to Lila. Meagan bounces her knee across from mine. She almost seems a little bored. Even though I'm happy to be sitting here, I can't stop thinking about how weird it must look from the outside—five girls and a boy.

We sit with them every day that week, but I hardly say anything. It kind of surprises me to hear all of them, but especially Lila and Amelia, gossiping about kids from our class. I wonder if, before Amelia and I joined them, they ever used to talk about me.

☆

On Friday after dinner, the phone rings. It's Amelia.

"Hey, Grayson," she says. "Do you mind if we don't go to Lake View tomorrow? It turns out there's something else I have to do."

I swallow hard. "Oh. That's okay," I tell her, trying not to sound disappointed, as I walk quickly to my room with the phone. I close my door. "Do you want to go Sunday instead?"

There's a pause. "Um, I think my mom said my aunt and uncle are coming to town to visit us on Sunday, but I'm not sure."

"I guess we could just go next weekend," I tell her.

"Okay," Amelia says. "Sorry about that. So, have a good weekend. I'll see you at school, okay?" I lean back on my bed.

"Sure, great," I tell her, staring at my blinding white ceiling. We say good-bye, and I hang up and throw the phone onto my pillow. I try to tell myself it's not a big deal, it's just one weekend, but disappointment settles over me like icy snow. I look at the bird in Mom's painting. I try to focus on it to keep myself from crying.

Chapter 9

IT TURNS OUT that I wouldn't have been able to go with her anyway. The next morning, Uncle Evan comes in just as I'm waking up to tell me that Grandma Alice is dead. "Adele told me that she went very peacefully in her sleep," he says as he sits on the edge of my bed.

"Oh," I say, because I can't think of anything else. I think of her soft hands and blue eyes.

"I just got off the phone with the funeral home. We'll bury her tomorrow. Okay?" he says, watching me carefully. I feel like I should be doing something, like crying, but all I can do is nod.

Uncle Evan waits for a minute before saying, "Okay," one more time. "So, if you don't want to talk, I guess I'll give you a little space. Aunt Sally and I are in the dining room if you need us." He gets up and watches me for a few more seconds before gently closing my door.

I look at Mom's smiling face in the picture next to me. Her hair is blowing around her cheeks. On my bookshelf with my old toys and books from Cleveland are the framed pictures: the blue house, Dad holding me outside of my preschool, Mom pushing me in a swing at a park. I get out of bed and look at them, one by one. I keep waiting to feel sad about Grandma Alice, but I can only think of Mom's face, and how, if she got to be a grandma, she probably would have looked just like Grandma Alice did.

The truth is that Grandma Alice had been pretty confused for as long as I could remember. It had been years since we really talked when I visited her. Mostly I'd just sit in her rocking chair and draw while she wiped down the clean countertops over and over again.

I guess there *were* those really thin lemon cookies that we used to eat together at her kitchen table when I was younger. I remember them now. And the narrow tin of freshly sharpened colored pencils that Adele always had ready for me. And there was the way the sunlight would come through the thin, waving curtains in the summertime when the windows were open. The gross nursing home smell would blow away, and the light would paint waves on the dark blue rug. They would move whenever the wind rustled the curtains. I used to bring my stuffed animals in my backpack, and Grandma Alice and I would sit in the middle of the waves and pretend my teddy bears were swimming all the way across a rough, giant ocean.

I'd kind of forgotten about that until now.

I don't want to go to the funeral, but in the end, Aunt Sally and Uncle Evan convince me that it will be okay. It's freezing at the cemetery and the sky is gray. I stand between them in the swirling snow and watch Grandma Alice disappear into the ground.

Chapter 10

ON MONDAY MORNING I sit in Humanities, organizing my notebooks and folders and watching everyone file in. I keep thinking about Grandma Alice's coffin being lowered into the dark hole. I'm looking for Amelia, and finally, just as the bell is about to ring, she walks in with Lila. I wave to her, but she doesn't see me. The two of them are too busy talking and smiling at each other, and, as they come closer, I notice that they're wearing almost identical outfits.

Their sweaters and skirts are crisp and new looking. The skirts flow to the ground, and the deep-red fabric looks bright against their black Uggs, especially Amelia's brand-new ones. The skirts are made of thin, gathered fabric that swishes and flows as they walk, and looking at them makes me remember

Grandma Alice's curtains in the summertime. And the purple skirt at the Second Hand.

I stare at my fingernails as Amelia walks over to our desks. I think of her phone call and how she said there was *something else* she had to do on Saturday. My brain races faster than my mouth can work. "Hey, Amelia" is all I can manage to get out.

"Hi!" She's whispering now under Finn's voice. "Did you have a good weekend?"

How could she just ditch me for Lila and then pretend that nothing is wrong? I'd been planning to tell her about Grandma Alice, but I just force a smile and nod. Luckily, I don't have to talk anymore because Finn is telling us that he's giving us quiet, independent work time all week since our big papers are due on Friday.

I take out my notebook, but I can't concentrate. I wonder if Amelia and Lila will spend every Saturday together from now on. I'll be stuck at home, doing nothing, just like before. And now I can't even go to the stupid nursing home to visit Grandma Alice. I think about the funeral, about how it was only the five of us and Adele there, and I realize that I'm the only person left from Mom's side of the family.

I feel like I'm disappearing.

Once fifth period comes, I know I can't go to the lunchroom. The thought of listening to everyone talk about their weekends and sitting there with Amelia and Lila in their matching skirts—the skirt that Amelia ditched me to buy—seems completely unbearable. I turn toward the library instead.

Walking through the wooden library doors at lunchtime feels strange, but also familiar. Mrs. Millen looks surprised to see me. She's sitting at her desk, eating a steaming bowl of some sort of Weight Watchers meal, just like she's been doing for years.

She puts her fork down when I walk in. "Hi, Grayson!" she says, studying my face. "Are you back to have lunch with me today?" She takes a sip of her Diet Coke.

"Yeah," I mumble, and hoist my backpack onto a desk. I sit at the empty cubicle next to it and unzip the outside pocket. I'm not hungry, but I take out my lunch bag anyway and let it thump onto the desk. I rest my chin in my hands and avoid Mrs. Millen's gaze. I wonder if the girls will ask one another where I am, and if they'll even care that I'm not there. Maybe they'll be glad I'm gone: the freak boy who eats with the girls. Amelia was probably just hanging out with me this whole time until she could find *better* friends—*girl* friends. I'm such an idiot.

I try to calm myself down. *It's not a big deal,* I tell myself. *You've eaten in here for years.* I stare at the cubicle walls where kids have carved their names into the wood. I never understood what would make someone do something like that, but suddenly, I want to take out a pen and do it, too. I picture the carving, *Grayson was here,* and I unzip my pencil bag and glance over at Mrs. Millen. She's still watching me curiously and she gives me a little wave, so I zip the pencil bag back up and squeeze my hands between my knees.

There's old tape stuck onto a wall of the cubicle in the shape of a smiley face. A wad of pink gum is shoved into one of the corners, and, right in front of me, hangs a crooked flyer. I look at it. MIDDLE SCHOOL SPRING PLAY TRYOUTS! it says in red computer print. There's a dumb picture of an opera singer underneath the heading. I keep reading.

WHEN? MONDAY AND TUESDAY, DECEMBER 15TH AND 16TH, 3:15–5:30.

WHERE? AUDITORIUM

WHAT? *THE MYTH OF PERSEPHONE*

SIGN UP FOR TRYOUTS OUTSIDE OF MR. FINNEGAN'S OFFICE

COME ONE, COME ALL!

I stare at the flyer. We learned about the Greek gods in fifth grade. Aunt Sally and I made flash cards together before my test, with the gods on one side and a description of each one on the other. I think the myth of Persephone is the one about how the seasons were created, but I can't remember for sure.

My mind wanders to the kids who have always done the plays and musicals at Porter—mostly older kids who are seventh and eighth graders now. Then I think about the quiet, kind of weird kids who do crew. I can picture them sneaking around behind the scenes dressed in black, invisible. Maybe I could do crew. But my mind shifts back to all the plays I've seen, to the spotlight, the deep burgundy velvet curtain and the solid, wooden stage. And to how it might feel to have everyone watching you.

I picture Amelia sitting at the lunch table this very second, laughing at every stupid thing that Lila says, and then I picture the empty place next to her, where I sat. I feel like a ghost.

I stand up, grab my uneaten lunch, and throw my backpack over my shoulder. I burst through the doors into the empty hallway, leaving Mrs. Millen and her Weight Watchers meal behind me.

The hallway on the fourth floor is dark and empty. Finn's office is the first one on my right and a piece of paper is taped neatly to the closed door. TRYOUT LIST FOR *THE MYTH OF PERSEPHONE* is printed along the top. I scan the list quickly for an open slot until I get to the very end. The last line is the only one that's empty: 5:15–5:30 on Tuesday.

A blunt pencil is dangling from a piece of yarn that's taped to the sign-up sheet. I pick it up and dig my fingernails into the worn, yellow paint. I study the imprint of my nail—proof that I'm still here—and write *Grayson Sender* on the line. When I drop the pencil, it sways like the pendulum on Aunt Sally and Uncle Evan's grandfather clock as I walk away.

I watch for Amelia at the bus stop after school. Eventually, I see her walking quickly over to me, her skirt bright against the thin layer of snow covering the ground.

"Hey, Grayson," she says, her breath thick in the icy air. "God, it's freezing out. Where were you at lunch today?" I study her face as she tucks her hair behind her pinkish ears. She's so clueless.

"I just had a lot of homework," I tell her, hiding my frozen hands in my jacket sleeves. "I went to the library." I can't bring myself to say anything more.

"Oh," she says. "Were you working on the Humanities paper? That's going to take forever to write."

"Yup," I say, relieved to have the excuse. "I might go to the library all week to work on it."

The bus pulls up, and Amelia and I get on. She runs her fingers over the creases in her skirt as we bounce along. At the Randolph stop, we say good-bye. I cross the street and don't look back.

☆

That night, I'm jittery. I've never tried out for anything before, and I have no idea what I'll be asked to do the next day. In first grade, our class put on *The Lorax*. Everyone had a part, and Emma and I were pink trees. I don't remember much about it except for the two of us standing together in the background. This play won't be anything like that.

Jack used to do the plays in elementary school. He's supposed to be helping Brett with his homework, but he's watching TV in the living room. I guess I could ask him about tryouts, but I don't want to. Aunt Sally and Uncle Evan are downstairs in our storage room organizing the boxes of Grandma Alice's stuff from the nursing home, so I can't ask them. Anyway, I don't feel like telling them I'm auditioning, so I just pull out my sketch pad and try to concentrate on my drawing.

The next morning, as Finn promised, we have the double period to work on our papers. I wonder if he noticed my name on the tryout list. I know I should speak up and just ask him what I'm going to have to do. So when the bell finally rings, I leave Amelia packing her things and stop in front of his desk.

"Grayson," he says, "I was just about to ask you to stay behind for a minute."

"Okay," I say. The class is gushing through the door now, and I look down. I study my shoes as the voices and laughs drift into the hallway. The classroom is almost still and silent now, except for the echoes of other kids' voices and a freezing breeze that has suddenly appeared. I look behind me. Somebody must have cracked one of the windows open at the back of the room and the cold breeze is rustling the poems and stories that Finn has tacked to the bulletin board on the wall.

"So, Grayson," Finn begins, leaning toward me a little bit in his chair. I watch his hands as he fiddles with a pen, and when I look up to his face, I see that he's smiling at me. "I saw that you signed up for auditions. I was really, *really* happy to see your name on that list. I'm wondering," he continues. "Can I ask what inspired you to try out? I mean, don't get me wrong, I think you'll be great on stage. Theater seems like an amazing fit for you, actually, but I'm curious. You've never shown an interest in any of the plays before."

I shrug. He watches my eyes, still smiling, and I don't know what to say. I picture the walls of the wooden library cubicle—old, dirty, and engraved with carvings of other kids' names. "Um," I stumble, "I don't know. I guess I just felt like joining an activity." I probably sound like an idiot, but he's still leaning forward, listening. He waits, but I don't know how to put it into words: how Amelia ditched me, and Grandma Alice died, and how I wanted to carve *Grayson was here* into the cubicle but I couldn't, so I signed up for play tryouts instead.

"Well," he finally says, "I think it's great. The play that I chose for this year's performance is magnificently written. It's really something special, so it's a good year for you to come aboard." I think about how cool that would be—to be a playwright and to get to decide what happens to all of the characters. The thought makes me smile. Finn is still looking at me eagerly, like he's waiting for me to say something else.

"I guess I just wanted to ask you what I'll have to do at the tryout," I finally say. The second bell rings and I jump.

"I can give you a pass. Don't you have study hall third period?"

"Yeah," I tell him, smiling. I drop my backpack at my feet.

"Great. It's very simple," Finn says, taking a pad of hall passes out of his top drawer and setting them on his desk. "When you signed up, you took a packet from the folder outside my office door, right?"

I swallow hard. "A packet?"

"Not to worry, not to worry." He rummages through his desk,

takes out a red folder, and hands me a thin, stapled packet from inside it. He must have read my mind because he says, "You definitely don't need to have anything memorized. There's a brief synopsis on page one followed by some one-to-two-page excerpts from the play. They're labeled with each character's name. During study hall or lunch, just read through them all and choose who you want to try out for. We'll have copies of the script on stage, or you can read from the packet when you come up to audition."

He pauses. I must look nervous because he says, "Grayson, your ability to analyze text and understand characters is excellent. Read the parts. Choose the one that feels right. I know you'll be able to do a very thoughtful reading."

I glance at the hall passes. Study hall is such a waste of time. "What's the play about?" I ask.

"It's a mythological story. Do you remember Persephone from your unit on the Greek gods last year?"

"Sort of," I say. "It's about how the seasons were created, right?"

"Exactly. In this version, Persephone is a girl who's about your age. She lives with her mother on Mount Olympus until she gets kidnapped by Hades, the god of the Underworld. The play *is* about how the seasons came to be, but it's also the story of her struggle to return home."

I nod. "And anyone can try out for any character?"

"Absolutely!" He looks over at the clock, puts my name and

the time on the hall pass, and rips it off the pad. "Here you go," he says. "And, Grayson?"

I take it from him. "Yeah?"

"I'm glad you're trying out. I know it's not easy to do something new." I pick up my backpack and try to picture myself on stage.

"Thanks," I say to Finn, and I smile at him and at the thought of not disappearing again.

Chapter 11

WHEN THE THREE o'clock bell rings, I throw all my books into my backpack and grab my jacket from my locker. The halls are bustling, and I'm surrounded by people as I make my way to the auditorium. I feel like I'm swimming in a crowded school of fish.

The giant room is empty when I arrive, except for some commotion behind the curtain on the rounded wooden stage, so I sit in the front row of fold-down chairs and flip through the packet Finn gave me. I've already read through the whole thing three times, but I flip through it again anyway.

The thick velvet curtain is partly opened, and I can hear Finn's voice from behind it. "I think I want to rearrange this today," he's saying. "I prefer the chairs on the opposite side, and this long table over here."

"I agree," a woman's voice answers, and furniture rattles across wood.

Some other kids start to file in. Most take seats near the back of the auditorium, but a few make their way over to where I am. I think again of *The Lorax*. I remember how the bright stage lights made it impossible to see the audience, and it felt like it was just the kids, all alone, up on the stage.

Andrew Moyer sits down right behind me. He's an eighth grader who has been a lead in every play I've seen for the past few years. I glance at his black T-shirt, open flannel button-down, and serious green eyes. Paige Francis and Reid Axleton, two more eighth graders, inch their way in next to him. I'm sure the three of them will get the biggest parts. I face forward quickly so they don't think I'm staring at them. They probably have no idea who I am, and I wonder if they think it's weird that I'm sitting up front, all alone.

Finn comes out from behind the curtain. He's disheveled looking, and he smoothes back his hair. When the noise in the auditorium dies down, he smiles at us. "Welcome," he calls out. Ms. Landen, one of the seventh-grade humanities teachers, comes out from behind the curtain with a microphone stand. Jack always says how much he hates her class, but she seems nice. She's smiling and young looking, and her long blond hair is pulled back into a low braid. She puts the microphone stand in front of Finn and hands him the mic. "Thanks, Samantha," he says to her back as she disappears behind the curtains.

"Welcome to play tryouts." Now his voice booms and fills every corner of the auditorium. Every crevice. My heart thumps. "I'm eagerly anticipating your auditions for *The Myth of Persephone* today. I am grateful to Dr. Shiner, as always, for supporting the arts programming here at Porter and for giving me the opportunity to direct this play."

Finn looks to the end of the front row of seats and smiles a stiff, polite smile. I glance over to see Dr. Shiner, the principal of Porter, sitting calmly in the last seat of the front row. His long, bony legs are crossed neatly, and his thin body looks like it has been swallowed up by his perfectly ironed suit. Everyone starts clapping, so I clap, too. Dr. Shiner stands and waves to the auditorium. His eyes are dark black, like they've sucked up all the color from the room.

Finn continues. "One by one, Ms. Landen and I will call you up for your audition. Once you're done, you're free to leave. All we ask is that you remain relatively quiet while you wait your turn. If you want to practice with a friend or talk softly, that's fine. We'll have the curtains partially drawn, which will block out a good deal of noise, but we can't have the volume level getting out of hand."

He looks around at us and smiles in my direction. I turn again to look at Andrew, Paige, and Reid behind me. "The cast list will be up on my office door Monday morning when you return from break. I want to stress to you," he continues, "that *everyone* will be cast in a role. There are many small nonspeaking parts in this play, between the Elves and the Souls of the Underworld, so if you want to be on stage for this performance, you will be. Nobody will be cut."

Finn takes the microphone off the stand and sits down on the edge of the stage with it. "And now for an extremely brief overview of *The Myth of Persephone,* for those of you who can't remember what you learned in fifth grade or didn't read the synopsis on page one of your packet." Andrew, Paige, and Reid giggle behind me.

"So, Persephone lives with her mother, the goddess of the harvest, Demeter. Her grandfather is Zeus."

"Zeus!" Andrew calls out in a loud, low voice, and everyone in the auditorium laughs. I turn around to look at him again. He's smiling at Finn.

"Moving along," Finn says, amused, "Persephone is kidnapped by Hades, the god of the Underworld. When this happens, Demeter becomes so depressed that all the crops begin to die." I think for a minute of Mom and Grandma Alice as Finn continues. "Zeus goes to Hades and tells him to free Persephone, which he does, and in the end, it's agreed that she'll spend half the year in the Underworld, at which time no crops grow, and the other half of the year with her mother, during which time the world will be in full bloom."

"And that's why we have the seasons!" Reid calls out.

"Exactly," says Finn.

He looks us over. "If there aren't any questions, we'll get

started." He waits for a minute and then nods at us. "Good luck to you all; I know you'll do great. First up, Andrew Moyer."

I look down at the packet in my hands. "Wish me luck," I hear Andrew say as he inches his way out. He leaps up the stage steps, two at a time.

I can't make out everything he's saying up there, but I hear him tell Finn that he's auditioning for Zeus, and I watch him take a red script from Ms. Landen. He flips through it, takes a deep breath, and starts to read. It looks like Ms. Landen is reading some of the lines, too, and I turn to page four in the packet, Zeus's part, and strain to hear what line Andrew is on.

I figured I'd try out for Zeus, but I know there's no way I'll get it over Andrew. He's older and taller and would obviously make a way better Zeus than me. I flip through the packet nervously and skim through the other parts again. I chew on my nail.

Up on stage, Andrew is handing the red script back to Ms. Landen. He takes a little bow and laughs, and I hear Finn tell him he did an excellent job. Paige scoots out behind me and grins at Andrew as she walks up the steps onto the stage. She seems so confident in her long, black skirt, shimmery with sequins, and I look down at my shiny black track pants that I used to be able to imagine so easily into a skirt just like hers.

Up on stage, she tells Finn she's reading for Persephone. Of course. I listen as she begins. Hades has kidnapped her, and she's demanding to be taken back to her mother. Her voice is loud and clear, and she sounds super dramatic. I look at the second page of the packet, at Persephone's part, and then around the auditorium again.

When Paige finishes, she and Andrew wait for Reid to audition before the three of them put on their coats and walk out the auditorium doors together. I glance at the clock on the wall and watch everybody in the room try out, one by one. I turn through the pages of my packet slowly. I should be rereading Zeus's part, but I can't focus on it.

It's almost my turn. My heart starts pounding, and when Finn finally calls my name, I'm the only one left except for two seventh-grade girls packing up at the back of the room. I watch them whisper and laugh as they put on their jackets and gather up their long hair, and I think about Lila and Amelia. The familiar longing races through my body—the familiar *wish*.

My heart thumping, I walk slowly up the stage steps and through the opening in the curtains into the small, makeshift room that Finn and Ms. Landen created. The auditorium doors slam as the two seventh graders leave. The lighting is dim on the stage, and the heavy burgundy velvet surrounds us. Finn and Ms. Landen sit behind the long table smiling at me, notebooks open to blank pages in front of them.

I try to smile back at them, but my legs feel suddenly weak, and now I feel like my thumping heartbeat is coming from somewhere else, somewhere outside of me. I look at the script that Ms. Landen is holding out to me. It looks like it's floating toward me. I take it.

"Grayson, you've been waiting forever," Finn says. He turns to Ms. Landen. "Samantha, this is Grayson, one of my sixth graders."

"Hi, there," she says, and I watch her write my name in her notebook. "Is this your first time trying out for a play?"

I nod and look down at the red script. *The Myth of Persephone* sparkles on the cover in shimmery gold writing. Beyond it are my black track pants and just one more time I try—I try to see them like Paige's sparkling skirt, but I can't. My heartbeat is like a drumbeat. It surrounds me. Each gentle thud creates ripples all around me.

I flip through the script. The word *Underworld* jumps out at me from the page, and I think of Grandma Alice's coffin, light brown and disappearing under shovelfuls of gray dirt and snow. I think of Amelia and Lila and their matching skirts, and of Paige's sequined skirt. And then I think, again, of my track pants.

"So, Grayson, who have you decided to read for?" Finn asks. His words come to me softly through the thick, warm air, and I look up at him, but I can't answer. All I can do, for some reason, is think about the years and years that I spend *pretending* my pants into skirts just like Lila's and Amelia's and Paige's, and how, for all those years, I just *pretended* that everyone else could see what I saw. And I think about how doing that used to make everything okay.

At home, my track pants and basketball pants hang in my closet, silky and shiny in a row of bright yellow, black, gray, silver, and gold, but they're only pants to me now. My too-long

T-shirts don't look like dresses. Without them, I'm nobody, and the idea takes shape in my mind. It takes shape and floats into my mouth, and it waits there.

I look down at my hands, at my chewed-up fingernails, and then back at Finn's face. The stage is silent and still. Finn and Ms. Landen are waiting for me to say something, so I do. I ask the question: "Can I try out for Persephone?"

Chapter 12

NOBODY MOVES and nobody says anything and my words hang in front of us like fog. My heart is pounding all around me. I watch Finn watching me, and Ms. Landen watching him. His face is calm, but he's studying me carefully now. I want to look down again, but I don't let myself.

He takes a deep breath. "Well," he says. And then he doesn't say anything for another minute. He picks up his gray pen and studies it, like he's trying to decide how to start the story that he's about to write.

I can't move, and I can't tear my eyes away from him and Ms. Landen. I don't know how much time passes, but it feels like forever. Finally, Finn opens his mouth to talk. "I suppose," he says slowly, like he's thinking aloud, "I suppose that there's no reason why you couldn't try out for Persephone." I nod. My heartbeat sinks back into my chest and I start to breathe evenly again.

"I mean, a tryout is just that, right? A *tryout*," he continues, and then he pauses again before saying, "What I mean is, yes, of course you can. Why shouldn't someone be able to try out for whatever character they choose? But, Grayson," he continues, looking at me carefully, "I should add: if we do feel that you're right for this role, we'd, well, of course we'd need to sit down and talk about things—about how people might react."

An image of Ryan's and Sebastian's faces pops into my mind, and my heart starts pounding again. I hadn't even thought of that, of what everyone else would think. "Yeah, maybe I—" But Finn's voice interrupts me.

"But it's premature to talk about that now," he says, and nods his head a final time. "Go for it, Grayson. Let's see how you do, reading for Persephone."

Persephone. I let the name bounce around my mind. I don't even want to imagine what people would say—a boy cast as a girl—and I think again of Ryan and Sebastian. And Jack. And everyone else, and for another second I think that maybe I should just try out for Zeus, or forget tryouts and join crew, but Finn's brown eyes are deep and kind. I'm frozen in front of the long table. And the faraway shadow of a hand from another lifetime has slowly rested itself upon my shoulder, like an echo. It smells like hand lotion and the clementine it just peeled and broke into pieces in front of me. *Stay*, it offers. I close my eyes for a second.

I see endless black dotted with glimmers of gold. I focus on them—on the sparkling lights, and then I open my eyes.

"What page?" I ask.

Ms. Landen looks at Finn one more time. He nods at her, and she clears her voice. "Twenty-seven," she says. "This is where Hades is trying to convince Persephone to be happy in the Underworld. We're having people who try out for Persephone—" She stops for a second and clears her throat again. "We're having you read this section because it's a part where Persephone shows a lot of passion and emotion, and we want to see how you would manage this intensity."

She opens her copy of the play. "I'm going to read for Hades. You may see us taking notes while you're reading. This is nothing to be alarmed about. You can start at the top of twenty-seven whenever you feel ready. And, Grayson?" she says.

I nod and swallow hard.

"Good luck."

I scan the words, and before I know what I'm doing, I start to read. Persephone paces around Hades's throne. She's peering out every window, one by one, and choking back tears. I envision myself in her shoes. It's not that hard to do, and I can practically see the dark gardens of the Underworld in front of me.

"'You must release me,'" I state firmly, finally turning to face Hades. I try to hide my emotion from him. Evil seeps from his menacing eyes, and I don't want him to think he has won.

"'My mother cannot exist without me,'" I read, but I know that what Persephone must really mean is *I can't exist without her,* and I hear my voice catch as I think of Mom's face in the picture on my nightstand.

"'Of course she can,'" Ms. Landen reads. "'And she will.'"

"'No.'" My voice is steady now, but I can sense Persephone's longing. "'I need to leave.'"

"'I will bring you everything you want,'" Ms. Landen states. "'Within reason, of course,'" she adds.

I look into Hades's cold eyes. "'My mother will figure out a way to come for me. Zeus will help her. Or I'll figure out a way myself.'"

Hades laughs a horrible laugh. I'm trying to scare him, but the truth is that his powers are much greater than mine.

"'Please,'" I beg. "'Just let me return home!'"

Hades grins, sensing his victory. And suddenly, I realize that I still have some control. I step forward, firmly.

"'All right, then.'" I make my voice cold, to match his. "'I will remain. But as long as I am here in this cold, dark, evil land, I will never smile. I will never eat. I will never do anything but try to get home.'"

Suddenly, Finn tells me I can stop. I look up from page twenty-eight of the script, and I feel almost surprised to be back in the burgundy room.

Finn and Ms. Landen stare at me and then, slowly, they look to one another, smiling. "Thank you, Grayson," Finn finally says, turning back to me. "That was very, *very* well done." In a daze, I hand him the script. He takes it, and for a minute, nobody says anything.

"So, I'll see you tomorrow morning in Humanities," he finally adds, and I nod.

I walk through the passageway in the curtains into the cold air. My eyes sting in the light as I walk across the stage and down the wooden steps. I gulp air awkwardly. I notice the hard floor beneath me. I feel like it's the first time my feet have touched the earth.

Part Two

Chapter 13

I GRAB MY STUFF off the seat where I left it. I don't feel like myself as I put on my jacket and backpack and walk out the side doors of the school and into the darkness. My breath is a puff of fog in front of me in the frozen air.

Across the street, I turn around and look at Porter. Most of the lights are still on inside, and the whole school practically glows against the black sky. The door of the east gym opens. A group of girls walks out, talking and laughing, and I wonder what time football practice will be over. I watch three teachers come out the giant arched front doorway holding overflowing tote bags. They walk down the steep steps to the parking lot.

I'm suddenly exhausted, but I force myself to think about what happened on stage. I try to remember exactly how I felt before I asked Finn if I could try out for Persephone, but it's a blur.

But then I think about reading Persephone's lines with Ms. Landen. That's not a blur. I can remember that; I remember how perfect it felt. I felt like I *was* Persephone, and I start to smile. The gym door opens again and a few more girls walk out, basketballs in hand. *That was very,* very *well done,* Finn had said, and it seemed like he meant it. And I felt that way, too. I felt like it *was* very, very well done.

There's a huge pile of snow next to the sidewalk behind me, and I run up it and jump off the other side onto the snow-covered lawn. "Yes!" I call out, and two old ladies walking down the sidewalk next to the bus stop look my way. I run across the snow, my ankles burning with cold, just as the bus pulls up. I skip up the steps. The driver is watching me with a little smile on her face. I look at her name tag. "Hi, Dori," I say. I wonder if she has kids.

She looks amused. "Good evening." I smile and sit down in the empty seat behind her. I plop my backpack onto the seat next to me, and think of Amelia.

Suddenly, I can barely breathe. *I just tried out to be a girl in front of the entire school.* I imagine Amelia, Lila, Meagan, Hannah, and Hailey at the lunch table, huddled together, their heads touching. I can practically hear their voices and laughter floating up from the jumble of headbands and braids and long, just-brushed hair—*He did* what? *What a freak.* I take my backpack off the seat next to me, hold it on my lap, and rest my head on it as the bus pulls away.

At home, the apartment is empty. I bring my backpack to my room, drop it on the floor, and look at myself in the mirror. I wonder what Finn and Ms. Landen saw at tryouts. I felt like I *was* Persephone. Did they see me standing there in front of them? Or did they see her?

I try not to let it, but the image of the girls' faces bursts into my mind again. Ryan and Sebastian join them, and Ryan's gaze stabs at me. I rub my eyes with my fists, hard, to create bursting firecrackers to burn the picture away. I should just forget about it and type my Humanities paper, but I don't feel like it, so I lie on my bed and try to think about the tryout and the feeling of *being* Persephone. I try to remember it exactly.

Eventually, I hear the front door open and close, and the sounds of Aunt Sally, Uncle Evan, Jack, and Brett in the other room. Jack pounds on my door and tells me it's time for dinner.

At the dining room table, I sit down next to Brett and scoop some takeout lasagna onto my plate. I'm too wound up to eat, so I push my food around while Uncle Evan reaches for the pitcher of water in front of me. "It's really too bad we couldn't make that trip to Costa Rica work, isn't it, boys?" He pours water into all of our glasses.

"Tell me about it," Jack says. "Every single one of my friends is going somewhere awesome. Did you know the Aarons are going to South Africa?"

"Huh," Uncle Evan answers, sitting back down and blowing on his lasagna. "Well, I'm sorry, guys. There was just no way. Not with the craziness that's ensuing at the office." He turns to Aunt

Sally. "At least you'll get some time off, huh, Sal? What are you going to do with yourself?"

"Now, there's the question," Aunt Sally says, chuckling. "I never know what to do with free time."

"So, how was school?" Uncle Evan asks.

"Whatever," Jack says. "It's almost break, so there's nothing much going on." I'm sure this is Jack's latest excuse for not doing his homework. For a second, I think back to his winning science fair project in fourth grade. The summer before school started, he set up all different kinds of birdhouses at Aunt Tessa and Uncle Hank's lake house in Michigan to see which ones the birds preferred. I remember them hanging in the overgrown rose bushes, little house wrens flying in and out of the tiny doorways. I try to remember exactly when Jack stopped caring about everything, but I can't pinpoint it.

"Brett? How was your day?" Uncle Evan probes.

"Good. It was good. Lucia spilled her water bottle on the computer table at After School Club and got in big trouble because you can't bring water bottles to the computer table. And there was an assembly."

"Is that right?" Uncle Evan asks him, and Aunt Sally smiles and leans over to cut up the green beans on his plate. "What kind of assembly?"

"I don't know. Some people in weird costumes with instruments."

"It was a string quartet from the Children's Symphony

Orchestra," Jack says quickly. "They did a holiday concert, but just for the elementary school."

Aunt Sally stops cutting Brett's food and looks up. For a second, she and Uncle Evan stare at Jack. "What?" he finally asks. "I saw a flyer in the hall."

Uncle Evan clears his throat. "Grayson?" he asks. "How about you? Anything interesting happen with you today?"

I hesitate and push my lasagna around my plate some more. I think of the soft curtains on stage and the warm, thick water-air. "I tried out for the spring play," I say.

Uncle Evan, Aunt Sally, and Jack stop eating and stare at me. They look stunned. Brett looks around at everyone. "What?" he asks. "That's cool, Grayson. We're doing a play soon, too." He looks around again. "What?"

A smile starts to creep across Jack's face, and I look back down at my plate. "Doesn't Mr. Finnegan direct the middle school play?" Jack asks.

"Yeah," I say. "So what?"

He shakes his head. "That guy is so gay." He's grinning like an idiot, and I have the sudden urge to get up from my chair and kick him. But I never would, so I dig my nails into the black leather seat instead.

"Jack!" Aunt Sally and Uncle Evan yell at the same time.

"What is wrong with you?" Aunt Sally goes on.

"I heard Mr. Finnegan's the best teacher in the whole school," Brett says.

"He is," I say, still staring at Jack. My ears feel like they're on fire. "The play he's directing? It's amazing. He's a genius."

"Whatever," Jack says, as he wipes his mouth with the back of his hand. "I'm sure it will be a snoozer." He looks at Aunt Sally and Uncle Jack, than back at his plate. He puts his fork down. "What's the big deal? All the school plays are."

"My goodness, Jack. Let's not forget that you were in almost every single play when you were in elementary school," Aunt Sally says. "You loved Drama Club." Jack rolls his eyes. Aunt Sally turns to me, smiling. "Grayson, I think it's great that you tried out. Don't you, Ev?"

"I do," Uncle Evan says, sounding proud. "I definitely do. So, when do you find out if you made it?"

My heart skips a beat. "Everyone makes it," I stammer quickly.

"I'm going to be the mayor in our play," Brett says. "When do you know what part you have?"

I can't talk about it anymore. "Monday after break," I tell them, pushing my chair back. "I have a big paper to type. Can I go to my room?" I ask. I put my plate on the kitchen counter and leave them and their curious gazes behind me.

The next morning in Humanities, I'm restless. One part of me feels like doing the mile run in gym, and the other part of me wants to go to the nurse's office and lie down on one of those little cots. I prop open my notebook in front of me and watch Finn at his desk at the front of the room. I scream silent messages to him: *I need this role!* Then my stomach drops. How could I be wishing for this? He looks up once and catches my eye. I feel my face flush and look quickly out the window. The old snow looks gray.

I watch Amelia out of the corner of my eye throughout the double period. She and Lila exchange looks and mouth words to each other. Amelia writes something in huge letters on a piece of notebook paper, rips it out, and holds it under her desk where Lila can read it from across the room. Lila starts laughing and buries her face in her hands. By the time the bell rings, Amelia's paper is still only half a page long.

I lean down to pack my backpack. "So, where were you yesterday?" Amelia asks me. "Did you get picked up after school?"

"Oh, no," I say, pretending nothing's wrong. I take a deep breath and look her in the eyes. "I actually tried out for the spring play."

Her face lights up. "Really?"

"Yeah, Finn's directing."

"I think that's great, Grayson!" she says. "I bet you'll meet a ton of new friends!" She swings her backpack over her shoulder and gathers her long hair in her hands. I swear, she looks relieved. "Will I see you at lunch? Or are you going to the library?"

"Library," I mumble as she walks to Lila's desk. I can't imagine ever sitting down with them at the lunch table again. When I pass Finn's desk, I avoid his eyes and walk out the door alone.

Chapter 14

I STAND, HUDDLED in the corner of the glass enclosure at the bus stop on Friday after school. Even though I can't stop thinking about whether Finn is going to cast me as Persephone, I'm glad that for two weeks I won't know. Everything feels hopeful and safe now, and I wish I could just stop time. I can't stand the thought of a crowd of anxious faces waiting to see the cast list on Finn's office door on Monday morning.

The wind is whipping like crazy. Amelia joins me at the bus stop. I don't know what to say to her. I know I'll never be able to tell her how I *really* feel about her and Lila's matching skirts. What could I possibly say: *I should have been the one wearing the same skirt as you*? I take a deep breath. I'll just be nice to her, I think. Nice, but not *too* nice.

She seems upset. "Are you okay?" I ask her.

"I'm so annoyed with Lila," she spits. "She told Asher that I have a crush on him."

"Oh. Do you?" I don't mean to ask the question, but I do. I feel like I'm covered in a layer of ice that is starting to melt. I can practically feel it loosening around me.

"That's so not the point. Since when are friends supposed to do things like that to each other? It's so obnoxious." She looks down the street for the bus.

"She probably just likes him, too," I say, pulling my hat down farther over my ears.

She glances at me. "I don't like him."

"Okay."

"I mean, I guess he's kind of cute."

I smile. I don't want to, but I can't help it. Amelia laughs a little as the bus pulls up. We get on together.

As we sit side by side, it starts to feel like fall again. I can almost hear dry leaves crunching underneath our feet on the sidewalks in Lake View. For a minute, I imagine the girls whispering at the lunch table again, but I force myself to stop. "Are you going away for break?" I ask.

"No, I was supposed to go to Florida with my dad and stepmom, but at the last minute they had to cancel. I guess she has this work thing."

"Oh." I wonder how stupid it would be to give her a second chance. "Do you have any other plans?"

"Not really," she answers. "Everyone's going somewhere."

"Yeah." I take a deep breath. "We should go to Lake View."

"Sure," she responds quickly. "Or, actually, we could go to this new thrift shop that my mom and I found in Wicker Park. It's kind of nicer, you know. I mean it's not so grungy. It's cool."

"Okay, great!" I say.

"So, do you want to go tomorrow? I think we took the 23. I have to ask my mom. But I can find out the schedule and call you later, okay?"

"Great!" I say again. "That sounds good."

The next morning I wake up to the sound of the wind whipping past my window. Outside, the ice on the lake is covered with fresh snow. A snowplow is making its way up the side street, but the sun is shining. It's already almost nine o'clock, and the bus leaves at nine forty-five. I take a quick shower and walk through the sleepy house to the kitchen. Aunt Sally is sitting on the love seat in the family room. She's wearing sweatpants and a T-shirt and reading something on her laptop. The muted TV is turned to CNN.

She pushes her reading glasses onto her head. "'Morning, Grayson," she says. "Did you sleep well?"

"Yeah," I say, glancing at the grandfather clock.

"You're taking a nine forty-five bus?"

"Yup."

"Okay. Are you sure you don't want to take a cab from Wicker Park afterward and meet us at the Planetarium? The timing would be perfect. Uncle Evan and I need a few more hours to organize the rest of your grandma's paperwork down in the basement, so we're not planning on getting there until eleven thirty or so."

Hearing Aunt Sally mention Grandma Alice makes me feel like leaving. "No, it's okay. I'll just come back here when I'm done. I don't know how long I'll be, anyway."

"Okay. Well, will you call my cell if you change your mind?"

I nod.

"You know, Grayson, Uncle Evan and I were talking last night after you went to bed," she says. "We're really glad you tried out for the play. Are you nervous?" She smiles gently.

Yes, I want to scream. *I'm dying. I don't know what I'm doing.* "Yeah. I guess two weeks is a long time to wait."

"It's almost cruel for him to make you kids wait all break!" She smiles again, but something snaps in me.

"He's not doing it to be cruel," I say quickly. "I'm sure he just wants to make a careful decision. He knows what he's doing, you know." And as soon as I say it, I wonder if it's true.

Aunt Sally looks a little hurt, and I look up at the clock again. I feel bad for her, but I don't know what to say. "I have to go," I tell her. "I have to meet Amelia."

"Okay, have fun," she says, watching me carefully. I walk into the kitchen and grab a granola bar and bottle of water from the pantry before I head out the door.

☆

The sidewalks in Wicker Park are covered in dirty snow. We get off the bus at the corner, and I follow Amelia half a block down the street to the thrift shop. The displays in the windows are bright and trendy looking. We arrive just as a lady is unlocking the door from inside and turning the CLOSED sign to OPEN. She holds the door for us.

"Good morning!" she says, smiling, as we walk in, and raising the blinds throughout the store. The countertops and tile floor glisten in the sunlight.

Two other saleswomen greet us, too. "Are you looking for anything in particular?" one asks. She's dressed neatly in a red turtleneck sweater, and her hair is wound into a tight, black bun.

"We're just browsing," Amelia answers expertly. She turns to me. "Our section is back here." She grabs my arm and guides me to a second room that's empty, except for us.

This store is definitely nicer than the Second Hand. There's a much better selection, and it seems cheerful. I don't know why, because the Second Hand is kind of gross, but for a minute I miss it—its familiar sloped, wooden floors and musty mothball smell. I think of all the time I spent looking for clothes in the boys' section—shirts that were too long or especially radiant.

I run my hands over the newer-looking clothing on the racks. I find a deep purple sweater that looks like it will fit and hang it over my arm. I roam around the quiet room and stop next to another rack.

I study the skirts in front of me and pull out a long one. *XS, $15.00* is written on the tag. I hold it up, close to my face.

The fabric is thin and creamy yellow. It looks like an antique. It's decorated with dainty embroidery and, around the bottom, tiny, amber beads hang delicately from a lace ribbon. I run the palm of my hand beneath them and smile. It looks like something Persephone might wear.

My mind wanders back to the deep-burgundy curtains on the stage, the warm, thick air, and the smooth indentation of the golden letters on the script. The rhythm of the drumbeat pounds distantly in my ears. I drape the skirt over my arm on top of the purple sweater and walk into a dressing room.

I hang the sweater on a hook on the wall. In the corner is a small stool covered in disgusting-looking green fabric. There's a rip on its surface where yellow foam pokes through. I put the skirt on top of the tear and take off my pants.

Amelia parts the curtains of the dressing room next to me. "Don't they have such a better selection?" she asks. I see her feet through the space below the thin divider that separates us. Her metal hangers clang on the hooks.

"Definitely," I tell her. I shake my damp shoes off my feet. A ball of icy snow on the tan carpet soaks through my sock. I'm in a daze. It's like I'm somebody else.

"My mom got an amazing dress here," Amelia says from her dressing room. I pull on the skirt and zip it up the side. It fits me perfectly. I take a step toward the mirror. The tiny beads tickle my ankles and make a gentle shaking sound, like two dice in a hand, or raindrops.

"Did you find anything good?" Amelia asks.

I pull my socks off. "Yeah," I tell her absently. I turn to see how I look from the side. The dice knock together again, softly. More raindrops and my beating heart. I look up. The mirror seems as tall as a building, and I suddenly feel like someone is behind me, but I can see there's only the beige back wall of the dressing room. I turn around to be sure, but I'm all alone.

I reach for the curtain. There's a bigger, three-way mirror on the wall next to the windows. All that exists now is me and this skirt, and I need to see how I look in the light.

The carpet is damp beneath my bare feet, but I don't mind. I stand in front of the mirror and examine myself. My hair is getting long. I lift up my white T-shirt so I can see the top of the skirt. It rests perfectly against my stomach. The lace is completely magnificent.

And suddenly, Amelia's image joins mine in the mirror. Her old socks are bunched around her pale ankles. She's wearing a blue jean jacket over her pink T-shirt and a long, flowery skirt. She's smiling. Her eyes glisten and dance. I don't breathe.

She throws her head back and laughs. Her hair swings behind her. "Grayson! What are you doing? You're hilarious!" I watch her eyes in the mirror as they travel down my body, and up again, from the amber beads to my eyes. I keep my eyes fixed on the image of hers as, with her grin fading, she scans my body, looking for clues. Our eyes meet again in the mirror.

Her face is suddenly serious. "Grayson," she whispers, "what are you doing?" She looks forward in the mirror toward the back of the store. I can hear the saleswomen in the distance. We stand side by side, staring at each other. She pushes her hair out of her face. "What are you doing?" she asks again. "Do you want people to think you're crazy?" I can't move.

"Grayson!" she whispers.

I think of Lila's crimson skirt. That should have been my skirt. I turn and look at Amelia, at her wide eyes and pale, freckled skin. Her voice returns to its normal level, and she looks out the window. "So, I better get home," she says. "There's a ten-thirty or an eleven o'clock bus, but I told my mom we wouldn't be long, so I better head out."

"Okay," I tell her. I can barely feel my own mouth forming the words.

She looks at her feet. "So are you coming, or are you staying longer?"

"I'm coming."

We change into our own clothes quickly. I leave the skirt in a heap on the dressing room floor, and we walk outside into the freezing air.

It's snowing again by the time we get on the bus, and we sit next to each other, looking ahead. My fingers and toes are freezing, but the back of my neck is on fire. I can't get the image of a cast list on Finn's office door out of my mind. Suddenly, I can't bear the thought of getting the role. But when I think of *not* getting it, I can't bear the thought of that, either. I wonder if I'm getting sick, and I rub a circle on the window. I need to see out, but it immediately fogs up so I stare at the cracked blue seat cushion in front of me instead.

We ride in silence, and I think about how loud the quiet is; I think about what it means. Finally, the bus slows to a stop on Randolph. I'm desperate to get off, but I can barely bring myself to move. My legs ache, and I know everything is over. Even if Finn doesn't cast me as Persephone, Amelia will tell the other girls. They'll be talking about me at lunch, about the boy who tried on a skirt—a beautiful, beautiful skirt. The gossip will spread down the lunch table like a disease, and nobody will ignore me again.

I stumble off the bus and walk across Randolph. Snow blows down my collar. I picture it turning to steam on my burning neck.

Chapter 15

THE DOORMAN opens the glass doors for me, and I stagger through. I immediately see Aunt Sally and Uncle Evan across the lobby standing close together, waiting for the elevator. Uncle Evan is holding one of those big manila envelopes, and they're talking excitedly.

I take a deep breath and try hard to pretend that everything is normal, but I feel wobbly when I walk. I can't stop thinking about Amelia's eyes staring at me in the mirror. "Hi," I say softly, coming up behind Aunt Sally and Uncle Evan. They turn around quickly.

"Grayson, you're home already!" Uncle Evan says, and they look at each other, smiling. I watch their eyes wander to the envelope in his hand. There's a *ding*, and the elevator doors open. I'm boiling, and I take off my jacket. Inside, Aunt Sally pushes the button, and we start to move.

"What's going on?" I ask, studying their strange-looking grins. Just talking makes me tired, but I try to act normal. I try to block out everything that just happened.

Aunt Sally gives Uncle Evan a little nudge. "Well, ah, we found something in your grandma's things that you're going to be *very* interested in," Uncle Evan says. My heart leaps, and my face feels even more flushed than before.

"What?" I ask. "What is it?"

"Look," Uncle Evan says, and he holds out the envelope. I reach for it. On the outside in red pen it says *Letters from Lindy (Save for Grayson)*.

I can feel sweat on my forehead now.

"Your grandmother obviously put these aside for you," Aunt Sally says, beaming. "Probably a long time ago. Can you believe it, Grayson?"

The doors open, but I can hardly move. Aunt Sally puts her hand on my back, guiding me out of the elevator.

"Grayson, honey," she says suddenly, stopping in the hallway. She studies my face. "Are you okay? You feel warm!" She holds her hand over my forehead. I think again of Amelia's wide eyes and clutch the envelope in my hand. *Letters from Lindy.*

I want to lean into Aunt Sally's hand. But instead, I tell her, "I don't know. I feel weird." My eyes are hot. I look at the envelope. I turn it over in my hands. "Where was this?"

"Is he okay?" Uncle Evan asks, touching my forehead. "I can't tell. Is he warm?"

"Where was this?" I ask again.

"Honey, it was in your grandma's files, the ones that Adele packed up for us." Aunt Sally fumbles with the keys and unlocks the door. "Get out of those wet clothes and we'll talk about it. We assume your grandma must have put those aside for you before she got sick. We were going to read them, but we decided not to." She pauses. "They belong to you."

I feel like I'm floating across the hall. I stare at the envelope, at Mom's name, *Lindy*, written in Grandma Alice's wobbly cursive, and I stumble to my room. My footsteps don't match the swish of surroundings passing me by and my legs don't feel like mine. I take my damp pants off, leave them in a pile on the floor, and get into bed. My feet are icy between the cold sheets.

I lay the envelope in front of me. My heart thumps, and my eyes burn. The door opens slightly, and Aunt Sally pokes her head in. Uncle Evan is behind her. "Can we come in?" she asks.

I nod.

Aunt Sally has a thermometer in her hand. "Open," she says. I do, and Uncle Evan sits on the foot of my bed.

"We're happy to read those with you if you want," Uncle Evan says. "We know it will probably be strange for you—"

The thermometer beeps, and Aunt Sally takes it out of my mouth. "It's slightly high, but barely," she says, and looks at my eyes again. "Grayson, how was your morning with Amelia? You're home awfully early."

I look away from her, at the painting on my wall. I focus on the bird. "It was fine," I say.

She pauses, and I can feel her watching me. "Okay," she says. "Should we read those letters with you? We know it might be difficult."

"No!" I say quickly, and I pick up my envelope. "No. It's okay. I'll be okay." I'm suddenly desperate for them to leave me alone.

"All right," Aunt Sally says. Uncle Evan gets up off my bed. "You'll let us know if you need anything?" he asks.

I nod, and they close my door behind them.

I turn the manila envelope over in my hands a few times before I open it and slowly tip the contents onto my bed. Three light blue envelopes slide out. They're addressed to Grandma Alice. I run my fingers over the handwriting, squint at the dates stamped over the postage stamps, and put the letters in order from the first one written to the last. I line them up neatly, their corners touching. I realize I'm not breathing and I force myself to.

I pick up the first envelope and turn it over. The return address on the back is our blue house in Cleveland. Grandma Alice didn't open the sealed flap. There's a neat, even slit across the top. I can imagine her slicing it open with the shiny metal mail opener that she kept in her kitchen drawer, and I wonder where that letter opener is now. The flap is licked shut. I know it's Mom's spit on the envelope. I run my finger along it, tearing open the flap. I close my eyes. I try to feel her.

Suddenly, it's like I'm floating, cross-legged, on my bed. I can't hear the TV or footsteps in the other room anymore, and everything is black. I feel the envelope, sturdy and thick. I open my eyes and peek inside.

The paper is pink inside the blue envelope. It's bright, almost fuchsia, and I pull it out. Tucked inside the paper are some photographs. There's a sudden crack in the blackness, and I feel like someone is watching me. I look at the door, but nobody's there. I unfold the paper and take out two pictures. I put them in front of me, one by one.

Once, at Tessa and Hank's lake house, I let myself sink to the sandy bottom in the shallow end of the lake. I plugged my nose and crossed my legs and opened my eyes. All around me was dark green and brushstrokes of light. The sound of nothing was very loud. It's what I hear now. I'll look at the pictures first, just for a minute. Then I'll read the letter, I tell myself. Then look at the pictures again.

The silence is roaring in my ears. I scan the pictures, not wanting to see too much yet. In the first one, Mom is holding a baby in a hospital bed. It's me. Her hand is cupped around my tiny back. In the other one, I am a little kid, looking up at the camera. My face is crisp in a surrounding blur.

I clutch the pink paper. My hands are sweating and I'm sure I'm wrinkling it, but I know Mom wouldn't mind. I open the card. On the top is says *September 6* and I look back to the date marked on the stamp. Mom wrote this almost exactly a year before the accident.

September 6

Dear Mom,

How are you? I miss you and hope you're well! Today's the big day—Grayson's first day of preschool! I'm a little nervous about it, but I'm sure he'll be fine. They have plenty of dress-up clothes and art supplies, so what could go wrong, right?!

Here are copies of the pictures I told you about. His teacher said they'll be working on the "All About Me" books for a while, but when he brings his home, I'll make a copy and send it to you right away.

Enjoy the pictures! Sending love from us all!

XO, Lindy

I put the pictures next to me. The air feels too thick. I want to read the other letters before I look at them again. Mom chose them. I want to save how she saw me for last.

I try to smooth out the wrinkles I made on the pink paper, and I put it back into the envelope. My hand is shaking as I open the second one. Inside is another bright pink card. The front of it is covered in purple scribbles. I unfold it carefully.

December 30

Dear Mom,

Grayson wants to say thanks for sending him the fantastic book of Greek myths for children! Can you read what he wrote? (Ha!) I'll translate: "Gran, Christmas book, thanks!"

In all seriousness, he absolutely loves it. He begs me and Paul to read it to him all the time. Actually, that's not accurate—he begs us to read him one of the stories over and over. He's completely obsessed with "Myth of the Phoenix." So much so that I'm going to add a phoenix flying above the earth in the painting I told you about. I'm finally almost done with it!

Thanks, Mom! Love you!

XO, Lindy (& Grayson)

I look up at Mom's painting—at the red, yellow, and blue bird that I've been staring at for all these years. It's a phoenix. I remember the story from fifth grade. I imagine a bird bursting into flames, its ashes in a heap on the floor until they finally take the shape, like magic, of another bird. My eyes are on fire. I can picture Mom's hand holding a small, wooden brush and dipping it gently into the red, then yellow, then blue paint to create it. Did she use a palette to hold the colors? Paper cups? I want to hold her hand. I want to study its creases and paper cuts.

But obviously I can't, so I pick up the last blue envelope that Grandma Alice put aside for me. It feels like there's another photograph inside, and I pull out the last pink card. The picture falls onto my lap, face up.

In it, my eyes are bright. I'm in front of a mirror. I'm wearing a pink tutu.

September 3

Dear Mom,

Here's the fantastic picture I was telling you about. Doesn't he look adorable? Thanks for talking to me last night. I know, in my heart, that Paul and I are doing the right thing, but it's been so hard for the past year since Grayson started going to school. I feel like we're always being judged for how we allow him to dress.

What you said the other day is true: Grayson is who he is. If he continues to insist that he's a girl, then it's our job to support him. All I want is for him to be true to himself.

Anyway, thanks for continuing to keep this quiet. Paul and I both still want Grayson to have the power to show the world who he is—whoever that may be—on his own terms and in his own time. Sending hugs and kisses.

XO, Lindy

Chapter 16

DARKNESS IS MOVING IN, and now the room is too dark and too bright all at the same time. Someone is holding the paintbrush, and they're flip-flopping between the colors of the darkest night and the brightest day. When the light comes, the world is a crystal. I can smell the hand lotion and clementines again.

I stay in this world, and I study my pictures. I look at how Mom and Dad saw me, and this is what I see: I'm a baby in Mom's arms in a hospital bed. I try to feel Dad's hands; I know they're holding the camera. My eyes are slits, and I'm wrapped in a white blanket. Mom is looking down at me. Her eyes look tired and heavy, but her smile is huge.

In the next picture, it's just my face. I reach for Dad's hands again. I want to pry them off the camera and hold them. Light is flowing in from somewhere, and it makes my eyes bright blue and my hair blonder. My face is calm, like I don't care what anyone thinks. Beneath me, my shirt disappears into a blur of purplish blue and for some reason the thought enters my mind—the thought that this is the picture of what *could* have been.

When I look closely at the last one, I stop breathing for a minute. I'm in front of a mirror and in the corner of it a flash of light hides Mom's and Dad's faces. Dad is holding the camera, and Mom's arm is around his waist. My back faces them and, in the mirror, I can see my smiling face. I'm wearing jeans and a white T-shirt underneath a pink tutu. In my hand is a plastic wand, its silver streamers swaying.

I close my eyes now, and I let the memory come to me—the only whole and complete one that I've kept from my first life. I let it float out of the velvet-lined box where I've kept it, locked carefully in my mind.

Mom and I are on top of a grassy hill. There's an ocean below us, and hot, humid air holds us. I'm wearing red, yellow, and blue. The thick air is like warm water. It puffs out our shirts and lifts our hair. "Let go of my hand," Mom says. "Put out your arms. Maybe this is how it feels to be a bird."

Chapter 17

MY EYES ARE the first part of my body to start working again. I look at the outlines of things: a glass of water on my bedside table, but not the water inside; window frames, but not the windows; picture frames, but not the pictures.

Then sounds come. The phone rings far away. Voices, loud and hushed, all at the same time. "Mr. Finnegan, hello!" Aunt Sally's muffled voice rising and falling, then rising and rising. It pounds on my eardrums.

Long, gentle silence.

"Sally, we need to just talk to him about it." Uncle Evan. Did Dad have a similar voice? Doors closing. TV. Footsteps on wood. I'm back-floating in still, warm water.

It's like those first nights after I moved here, and I remember them now—the strange smell of the pillowcase, the sliver of light that fell through the opened doorway at night and how it bent over the corner of the bed and onto the rug and faded into darkness near the dresser, like a road to nowhere.

My body is burning. I'm asleep and awake all at once, and images come in snippets. The bedside lamp is suddenly on. I can see the light like an explosion through my eyelids. Paper rustles. Silence.

"Oh my God, Evan, read this."

Whispering. Paper unfolding, folding.

Someone sitting down, pressure on the bed, wire on foam.

"Look at this picture."

More rustling and the sounds of quiet and breathing.

Whispers again. "Oh my God, Evan. What do you think she meant?"

Nothing. "Evan!"

"It's perfectly clear what she meant, Sally. *Perfectly.*"

Silence.

I barely know if the voices are real. My blanket scratches at my neck. My feet can move now, and they kick the covers off. I open my eyes. Uncle Evan's face is close to mine. His gaze shifts from my eyes to my chin. His eyes are soft, and they study my face.

I see the tiles around the toilet now, gleaming—bright, clean white. I'm sick, and Uncle Evan's hand is on my burning back. The toilet is flushing. I look away and hold on to the sink. A cold washcloth is on my neck. It's like I'm sleepwalking, and I'm back in my bed, asleep in the darkening room.

But, eventually, I can tell that morning is coming. Someone has put the covers back over me, and the room is brightening. When I finally open my eyes, the first thing I look at is the phoenix flying in the painting over my bed. Nothing that happened feels real, but when I turn away from it, I see the three sturdy blue envelopes propped neatly against my lamp.

Chapter 18

I SIT UP SLOWLY. My mouth is dry, and my body is weak. I stare at the blue envelopes, and I can't believe what happened. It feels like a dream, but the envelopes are there, right in front of me. I pick up the last one, the one Mom wrote just before the accident, and I pull out the pink paper again.

Grayson is who he is, she said. Who am I? I want to *hear* her tell me. I look at the picture of me in the tutu. *All I want is for him to be true to himself.* My mind races, but I keep coming back to what I know is true: they knew. They knew, and it was okay.

I swing my legs carefully over the side of my bed and stand up. My blood rushes to my feet and I'm dizzy. I haven't had anything to eat or drink since yesterday morning. As I walk to my closet for a pair of pants, I see myself in the mirror in my white T-shirt and underwear, and I suddenly remember Amelia's dark eyes in the store mirror. Darkness starts to seep in again, and I turn back to my bed. The springs squeak as I sit down, and Uncle Evan's head pokes through the cracked doorway.

"Grayson? You're up! How are you feeling? Sally!" he calls. "He's up."

I hear quick footsteps, and Aunt Sally appears beside him. She takes a cautious step into my room. "Grayson!" she says. "Are you okay?"

"I think so," I tell her. But when I think about yesterday, feelings of sickness and dread come to me like words trying to make a sentence. I sit on my bed and watch Aunt Sally and Uncle Evan standing in the doorway.

"Grayson," Aunt Sally starts awkwardly. "Those letters. Uncle Evan and I read them last night. When we gave them to you, we didn't know. We didn't know what they'd be about." She looks down at her feet. "We should have read them first," she says, still not looking at me. "That must have been very difficult for you." Her voice fades away. "We're sorry." Uncle Evan is watching her. I wait for her to go on, to tell me what exactly she's sorry about, but she doesn't say anything else.

"Son, why don't you get dressed and come to the living room so we can talk?" Uncle Evan says. "Tessa came about an hour ago to take the boys to the lake house for the day." He glances at Aunt Sally uncomfortably. "And, well, there's one other thing that we need to talk about, too," he says, still watching her.

I can't feel a thing. Half of their words bounce off of me like light on a mirror. I pull on my pants and brush my hair. My face is pale, and I'm dying of thirst. I walk to the living room, numb, the feeling of cotton behind my eyes. I feel like I'm four again.

I sit on the couch across from them. On the end table next to me are a glass of water and a mug of tea that Aunt Sally must have made. I drink the water carefully and pull a red pillow onto my lap. I hold it there like a shield.

Uncle Evan runs his fingers through his hair, studies his hands for a minute, and begins to talk. "Grayson," he says, "I guess there are a couple of things we need to discuss with you."

I don't move.

"The first thing is that, like your aunt Sally said, we know it must have been very difficult for you to read those letters from your mom. We didn't know what they'd be about. And what your mom said, well, we're not quite sure what to make of it." He looks at me carefully. "Or what *you* make of it."

Nobody says anything. "You know," he finally goes on, "how she talked about wanting you to be who you are, and how she included that picture of you in the, uh, the pink dress," he says.

"Tutu," I correct, automatically.

"I'm sorry?" Uncle Evan asks.

"It's called a tutu."

"Right. Well. That was obviously a very long time ago."

I'm starting to feel sick again.

"And we don't have to talk about anything right now if you don't want to, but we do want you to know—Aunt Sally and I *both* want you to know that you can always come to us. With anything."

"Of course he knows that," Aunt Sally stammers quickly. I look at her flushed face and nod automatically. Uncle Evan watches me expectantly, but I'm frozen. The room is quiet except for the ticking clock.

After a minute, Uncle Evan clears his throat and continues. "Well, then. I know this is a lot—a lot to think about, and you probably feel very overwhelmed, but the other thing that we need to talk to you about, Grayson, is that yesterday when you were in your room, when you were, ah, reading the letters, Mr. Finnegan called."

A tiny wisp of memory of Aunt Sally's voice weaves its way back into my mind, and my heart starts to race.

"He called to ask us—"

"He didn't call to ask us anything," Aunt Sally interrupts. "He called to *tell* us."

"Okay, well, he called to say that he was thinking of—"

"Not thinking of, Evan. He had made the decision." I realize that Aunt Sally is fuming. Her face is hard, and her eyes are cold. I don't think I've ever seen her like this before.

I can't contain myself. "Why did he call?" I yell.

Uncle Evan looks shocked. "Well, apparently you tried out for the lead *female* role in the play, Grayson?"

My heartbeat is wild. I nod.

"Grayson," Aunt Sally pleads, her forehead wrinkled in concern, "why?"

"Take it easy, Sal," Uncle Evan says to her softly.

"I'm sorry," she continues. "It's just that, well, Grayson, I'm worried about you. Why would you want to set yourself up to be teased like that? Kids can be very cruel, especially in middle school. I'm just trying, Grayson, I'm just trying to protect—"

"But what exactly did he say?" I interrupt.

"Now, hang on a minute," Uncle Evan says. "We'll get there. But what Aunt Sally said—it *is* something to think about. If you want to do this, to play a girl's role, well, you should do it. That's how I feel." He looks at Aunt Sally. "But, Grayson, what your aunt is saying is true. Kids are not going to be kind about it."

"So, did he say—?"

"You know," Uncle Evan says, "we, ah, we didn't know until we read your mom's letters that you'd also been like that before you came to us."

"Also?" I ask.

"When you first moved here, you used to dress up as a girl all the time," Aunt Sally says. "I suppose that's what your mom was referring to in her letter."

I tighten my grip on the red pillow. "I did?" I ask.

Uncle Evan nods. "We didn't know what it meant." He pauses. "Your dad and I had grown apart quite a bit by the time you moved to Cleveland. It's one of my biggest regrets—that we didn't talk to each other more." He takes off his glasses and rubs his forehead.

"Oh," I whisper.

"But it was just for a little while that you dressed up," Aunt

Sally adds quickly. "Like your mom said, you actually insisted for the first couple of months that you lived with us that you *were* a girl. But your teacher, Mrs. Stern, assured us that it was all a normal phase, or possibly a reaction to the trauma, and that it would pass. And it did."

Uncle Evan looks at her. "It did, Sally, but only after we explained to him that Jack would stop tormenting him if he just acted like a boy." He turns back to me. "You used to wear my undershirts like dresses. They were way too long on you. You used to trip over them. I don't know. I suppose . . . Maybe we should have gotten you—"

"Evan!" Aunt Sally interrupts. "All it took for him to stop the behaviors was a simple explanation that this is not something that boys are *supposed* to do."

My hands are sweating. I swallow hard. "And then I stopped?" I ask.

"Of course you stopped," Aunt Sally says quickly. "You had no problem stopping."

"Well, Jack wasn't exactly easy on him," Uncle Evan says to her, as if I'm not sitting right across from them. "Maybe *that's* why he stopped. Maybe he didn't want to deal with Jack teasing him about it anymore." He pauses. "And you and I, well, it's not like we exactly supported Grayson the way it seems Lindy and Paul did." His voice catches when he says his brother's name.

Aunt Sally takes a deep breath. "It was a hard time for everyone." She turns and looks at me again. "Jack felt very displaced when you arrived. He was only five and a half. He didn't know right from wrong, and Brett was just a tiny baby. We had so much—"

Uncle Evan cuts her off. "Anyway, you and Jack eventually became great friends," he says. He glances at Aunt Sally, and it looks like he's trying to force himself to smile. "It just took a few years."

I stare at them. I feel like I've just read the prequel to my life story, like I'm understanding things for the first time. "Why didn't anyone tell me about this before?"

"Oh," Aunt Sally says, "I guess I thought you remembered."

I stare at her blankly.

"But, Grayson, the point is that we need to make a decision together here," she continues. "About whether or not it's a good idea for you to do this. To play the role of this, ah, Persephone character. Mr. Finnegan said he already cast you, but before making it official, he wants to confirm that you're still up for it. So we have a very easy opportunity to just tell him—"

"So I got the role?" I ask them, standing up. The red pillow falls on the floor.

"Yes, Grayson, that's the whole point," Aunt Sally says. She looks at Uncle Evan and back at me.

All of a sudden, I can't help smiling. I don't mean to, because Aunt Sally looks like she's about to cry, but I can't stop. I say it again, just to hear how the words sound one more time: "I got the role."

"This is completely ridiculous," Aunt Sally says, looking up at me, her voice rising. "Mr. Finnegan has absolutely no business putting you in a position like this!" Now she doesn't look like she's going to cry anymore—she looks furious again. Beside her, Uncle Evan seems small and defeated. He rubs his hands on his knees as he looks up at me. And even though all I can remember about Mom's and Dad's faces is how they look in pictures, it's like they're standing next to me now. Their hands are on my back, and I can't turn my thoughts away from a vision of myself on stage, in the spotlight, in a beautiful, flowing gown.

"Grayson, are you okay?" Uncle Evan asks, watching me strangely.

"Yeah," I tell him, still grinning. "I'm perfect."

Chapter 19

TESSA AND HANK drop Jack and Brett off after dinner.

"I hope you're not contagious," Jack says, passing me on the way to his bedroom. He slams his door. I think back to when we were younger and he would open his bedroom door for me when I did our secret knock—*tap, tap, bang, bang, bang.* I remember the time we went sailing with Tessa and Hank while Brett sat on the pier with Aunt Sally and Uncle Evan in the whipping wind and blinding sun. The sailboat capsized in the reeds on the far side of the little lake. Jack and I were laughing in the water, bobbing up and down in musty-smelling lifejackets. He reached for my hand and helped me crawl up onto the slippery, white bottom of the boat.

Brett looks down the empty hallway and then sits on the couch next to me. "Are you still sick?" he asks.

"Nope, I'm good," I tell him. I wonder what Aunt Sally and Uncle Evan told Tessa and Hank. They wave to me from the doorway. Do they know about the play? The thought horrifies me.

We sit on the couch together for the rest of the night. Even after it gets late, Aunt Sally and Uncle Evan don't make us go to bed. I pretend to be watching *Star Wars* with Brett, but really I'm lost in my thoughts. Whenever I used to imagine Mom and Dad, I'd think of their faces in the framed picture on my nightstand. But now it's different. Having those letters—now it's like I can actually *feel* them next to me.

Winter break drags on. I can tell that Aunt Sally and Uncle Evan are trying to give me space, but I catch them staring at me strangely all the time. Aunt Sally gets us a week's pass to the museums, but there's no way I'm going. Every day, she, Jack, and Brett head out after breakfast. I lie on my bed a lot and look at Mom's painting. I especially look at the phoenix. I read the letters over and over again. I study my pictures. Mom and Dad *knew*. They knew, and it was okay.

One night after dinner, Aunt Sally and Uncle Evan come in. "Grayson," Aunt Sally starts, "we just want to check in with you—to see how you're doing. And to see where you're at with this, ah, play thing. Mr. Finnegan left another message on my voice mail today. I think he really wants us to call him back."

I sit up in bed. "You haven't called him back yet?" I ask.

"Well, your uncle and I wanted to give things a little time. You know, to settle." She looks at Uncle Evan.

"So," he asks me, "are you still thinking that you'd like to take on the role?"

"Yes!" I say. "Definitely."

"Why?" Aunt Sally sounds desperate. "Why do you want to set yourself up to be teased? Other kids could make your life miserable if you do this, Grayson. You could get bullied. You could get *hurt*."

I don't feel like myself anymore; it's like I'm acting in a performance already. "I don't know," I say. "I guess it's just that I feel . . ." I take a deep breath and look at them. "I mean, I've been thinking about what you said, about how I could talk to you, and about how I was when I first moved here. . . ." They both stare at me frantically, their eyes wide. "I guess I still feel—"

"You feel *what*, Grayson?" Aunt Sally interrupts anxiously.

I look from her unblinking eyes to Uncle Evan's. "Nothing," I say, lying back down. "I just wanna do it. That's all. If I get teased, I can handle it." I have no idea if this is true.

"Well," Aunt Sally says flatly, "I think we should tell Jack and Brett. Just so they're prepared." She looks hurt and my stomach tightens. Prepared for what?

"Fine," I say. They stand there for another minute before closing my door.

☆

The next morning I stay in bed as long as possible. After a while, though, I know I need to get up. I'm starving, and I have to go to the bathroom. Besides, I can't hide out forever. I think of what Aunt Sally and Uncle Evan said about how Jack treated me when I first moved in. When I walk to the dining room, I feel myself bracing for an attack.

Aunt Sally, Jack, and Brett are at the table eating breakfast. "Hey! Look at the pretty lady!" Jack calls out. Brett watches him, his spoonful of cereal frozen halfway to his mouth.

"Jack, this is exactly what I'm talking about. You need to leave him alone," Aunt Sally warns, looking up from the paper. "How'd you sleep, Grayson?" she asks automatically.

"Fine," I tell her, watching Jack out of the corner of my eye. I sit down next to Brett and pour myself some cereal.

Brett turns to me, his mouth full now. "Dad told me the story about Persephone and why there are seasons," he says, chewing. "So, you're gonna be Persephone?"

"Yeah," I tell him, forcing a smile.

"Is it a true story?" he asks.

"Nah," I say. "It's made up."

He nods.

"Well, *Grace*, I think you'll make a perfect girl," Jack says. "But what am I supposed to tell all my friends when they ask me why my cousin is totally gay?" His face turns pink when I meet his eyes, and he looks down and plays with his cereal.

"Jack," Aunt Sally says sternly, but she sounds exhausted.

Brett watches us, confused, and I think again of how I'll look to everyone else, onstage, in a dress, and I understand, suddenly, that this question is out there, this question of what it all means. I think of what Mom wrote—*All I want is for him to be true to himself*—and in this exact moment I wish for her harder than ever before. I need her to tell me who I am. I need her to say it, because I know what Jack thinks, and I know it's not that.

"What does—" Brett starts, but Jack interrupts him.

"Well, what am I supposed to say to everybody?" He glares at me.

"I don't know," I mumble. Anyway, I *don't* know. "I'm sorry," I say.

"Well, obviously you're not sorry enough. If you were really sorry, you wouldn't do it. You're a total embarrassment."

"That's enough, Jack," Aunt Sally says quietly.

"Whatever," he spits. He gets up from the table and storms out of the dining room. I hear his bedroom door slam.

Brett looks back and forth between me and Aunt Sally. "I don't get it," he says. "Why can't Grayson be Persephone?" Aunt Sally looks out the window as Brett continues, "It's just a play."

Even though I want to, there's no way I can explain that it's so much more than that. Brett's words just hang there, half-true, in the air.

☆

That night, I lie awake in my bed in the dark. The house is still except for muffled voices coming from Aunt Sally and Uncle Evan's room. I look at my clock; it's almost eleven o'clock. I creep quietly through the hall and sit on the cold, wooden floor across from their closed door. They're arguing.

"Just tell me everything he said, Sally, for Christ's sake, without interjecting your opinion every second!" Uncle Evan is saying.

"Would you lower your voice? You're going to wake everyone up!" Aunt Sally replies in a loud whisper. "I just told him he had overstepped his bounds as a teacher, that's all. I told him that Grayson still wanted the role, but that no teacher, no *one person*, should be allowed to make a decision like this without a serious conversation with everyone involved!"

"And?"

"Then he said that he'd like to sit down with Grayson to talk about how people might react to everything, and to coach him through how he could respond. I told him no way, not to bother, that we were talking *all* about the possible ramifications at home."

"Sally, are you sure that was a good idea?" Uncle Evan asks. But it's like she doesn't even hear him.

"Then, he just said that he didn't mean to step on anyone's toes, but he believes that any teacher who is really going to make a difference in the life of a student is going to blur the boundary between the kid's academic and personal life. Or something like that. Utter nonsense. I told him he was creating a monster. This entire situation is spinning out of control, and I can guarantee you that Grayson is only going to get hurt as a result."

My heart is thumping. There's silence.

Finally, Aunt Sally starts to talk again. "I suppose we could just tell Grayson he *can't* do the play." My stomach ties itself into a blazing knot.

"No," Uncle Evan says abruptly. "Absolutely not. Grayson has not involved himself in *anything* for how many years? And then the first thing he finally decides to get out there and do, we forbid? No way." Aunt Sally doesn't respond. "Anyway," Uncle Evan continues, his voice quieter now, "I mean, maybe this whole play thing *means* something. Maybe the dressing up wasn't 'just a phase.' You read Lindy's letter."

"Of course it was a phase!" Aunt Sally replies quickly. "And who knows what *exactly* she was talking about. But you know what, Evan? Let's just say it wasn't a phase. That's not the point. It's not Mr. Finnegan's place to get involved. *That's* the point. He is completely inappropriate. I'm calling Dr. Shiner Monday morning. I'm sorry if you disagree, but I am. He needs to know how I feel about this decision. Maybe there's something he can do. Mr. Finnegan is setting Grayson up for something too big for anyone to handle. Grayson is a *child*—he's in no position to make a decision like this on his own."

The knot in my stomach tightens.

"God, I can just see Lindy encouraging this in him, you know?" she says.

"Jesus, Sally," Uncle Evan whispers.

"I'm sorry, Ev," Aunt Sally goes on, softer now. I strain to hear. "Honestly, I don't think I'm cut out for this type of thing." There's another long silence, and then she continues. "Remember that time when he first moved here and we all went to the Clarks' for dinner? Remember the kids were all playing dress-up, and we had to practically drag him out of Allie's dress to get him home? God, I just remember the way Alex and Esther were looking at us while he was lying on the floor screaming—like we were completely incompetent."

"Sally," Uncle Evan says again, even softer this time.

"Anyway," she continues, "he's going to get teased horribly. That's really the point."

I can't listen anymore, so I creep back to my bedroom and close the door quietly. My hands are shaking. I tuck my covers in tightly around me and shut my eyes against the darkness.

Chapter 20

AS I WALK UP the empty stairway to the fourth floor in the early morning winter light, I hear voices drifting through the closed door at the top of the steps. I already know my role. *So, why are you doing this?* I suddenly scream to myself. But, the thing is, I *want* to. I want to stand in a crowd, huddled at Finn's closed office door, reading the cast list, seeing who got what part.

I adjust my backpack and study the doorknob for a minute before I finally open it and walk slowly over to the small crowd of mostly seventh and eighth graders. Tommy is there, and Reid, Paige, and Andrew, of course. Meagan, Hannah, Hailey, and a few other sixth graders stand in front of the list, too, studying it, whispering and pointing. I didn't even realize they had tried out.

I inch my way into the crowd quietly and focus on the white paper on the closed doorway. I don't look at anybody, but I can feel everyone all around me. And there it is:

Persephone—Grayson Sender

Ink on paper. Permanent. My heart beats firmly, and I smile to myself as I read through the rest of the list:

Hades—Reid Axelton
Zeus—Andrew Moyer
Demeter—Paige Francis
Hermes—Tommy Littleton
Lead Elf 1—Meagan Lee
Lead Elf 2—Audrey Booker
Lead Elf 3—Natalie Strauss

I'm surprised to see Meagan's name as one of the smaller leads. She's so quiet in class. I wonder how she'll do. I scan farther down the list to the smaller roles, the other Elves and the Souls of the Underworld. I see that Hailey and Hannah are Elves numbers eleven and twelve.

I stare at the paper for as long as I can. A buzz of whispers surrounds me. I don't want to turn around, but I know I can't stay here forever. So I stuff my hands in my pockets, lower my head, take a deep breath, and turn to leave. I try to feel Mom and Dad next to me like I did at home over break, but I can't. I'm completely alone.

"Congratulations, Grayson." The voice sounds sharp. I cringe, thinking of Aunt Sally's warning, and look up. It's Paige. "It's pretty impressive that a sixth grader got the lead." She adjusts her backpack and folds her arms over her chest.

"Thanks," I say, forcing a smile. Reid walks over to us, and I feel like getting out of here fast, but Paige keeps talking.

"I thought that was going to be my role. Usually eighth graders get the leads."

"Oh." My face is hot. I don't know what to say. "Sorry, I, uh . . . I guess I didn't think I'd get it," I finally mumble.

She takes a deep breath and looks quickly up at Reid. "Well," she says, looking me over. It sounds like she's giving in. "I guess you better call me 'Mom' from now on."

The room wavers. Just once, and just for a second. I steady myself and focus on Paige's layers of brightly colored, silky shirts. A clump of tangled necklaces and chains hangs around her neck. Nobody else at Porter dresses like her. "Right," I say.

Andrew joins us. The three of them look at me curiously. "I better get to class," I say quickly.

"What do you have first period?" Andrew asks.

"Um, Humanities, with Finn."

"Best class *ever*," he says, smiling at me.

"Yeah, definitely," I say. "So, I better go."

"See you tomorrow at rehearsal," he calls as I walk to the staircase. Before I get to the doorway, I turn around and look at the three of them once more. Reid and Andrew are standing close together, talking quietly, and Paige is still staring at me. Then I see Meagan, Hailey, and Hannah off to the side, not saying a word, and I realize that they were probably listening to our conversation.

"Hey, Grayson?" Meagan suddenly calls. She glances quickly at Hailey and Hannah, and then back at me.

"Yeah?"

"Wait up; we'll walk with you. Come on, guys."

I almost tell them that I'm fine, that I'll just go on my own, but I don't. Hailey and Hannah follow her, and the four of us walk down the stairs to the first floor.

☆

I pause for a minute outside the door to Finn's room and watch Meagan, Hannah, and Hailey go in. I know Amelia will be inside. I wonder if she's told everybody about the skirt yet. The thought makes me hate her.

Finn isn't sitting on top of his desk, greeting everyone the way he usually is, and I realize how much I'd been looking forward to seeing him. I hunch my shoulders forward to try to make myself as small as possible as I walk to my seat.

Across the room, Amelia is sitting on Lila's desk. They're

laughing hysterically. Hailey joins them. "Hey, guys," I hear her say. "What's so funny?" I strain to hear them.

Amelia leans over toward Lila to whisper something in her ear, her hair falling across both of their shoulders. Hailey stands back a bit and watches. They could be talking about anything, I tell myself, but my heart is pounding.

Ryan and Sebastian sit down in front of me. Ryan turns around as Sebastian starts to unpack his backpack. "Hey, Grayson," he says in a too-sweet voice. Sebastian glances at him, and I stare ahead. I can feel my face turning red. "What'd you do over break?" He pauses. "Your auntie take you shopping for some new flannels?" He glares at my shirt. "Oh, you're gonna ignore me? What a shock."

Sebastian taps Ryan's shoulder and points to Finn, who is walking through the doorway, a stack of papers in his hands. He plops them onto his desk, smoothes down his hair, and looks us over.

"In your seats, everybody," he says above the talking and laughter. "Sorry I'm late. Welcome back, welcome back! I hope everybody had a relaxing break." The class quiets down and I keep my eyes fixed on Finn as Amelia takes her seat next to me. She doesn't say anything, and neither do I. Out of the corner of my eye, I notice that she's wearing a new bracelet. Tiny hearts dangle from a silver chain. For some reason, I want to touch it, but I never would.

"I know it's been a long two weeks, and your heads are probably still in the clouds, but I assume you all remember that before break, we completed our unit on the Holocaust," Finn says, smiling. "I'll return your papers at the end of class. Today we're going to shift gears. I want you out of your pairs and back into your original rows from first quarter. I've got new plans for us for this unit. So, let's get up and move. Try to remember where your desk was. If your memory has failed you, come see me!"

Everyone starts to rustle around. "As soon as you're back in your places, I'll pass out our new novel." He holds a copy of *To Kill a Mockingbird* above his head. "It's a difficult novel, but it's one of my all-time personal favorites!" He practically has to yell to be heard over the sounds of people talking and pushing their desks and chairs across the floor. I shove my desk away from Amelia's without looking back.

It's a relief to be away from her. I look around at the rest of the class and notice Meagan watching me with her almond-shaped eyes. She looks down when my eyes meet hers, but after a second, she looks back up and smiles. I smile back.

"Okay!" Finn shouts. "Quiet down! Let's get started! We're going to jump right in. Notebooks out!" He scribbles *To Kill a Mockingbird* on the board. I copy it down in my notebook and sketch a princess as I listen to him talk. I study her for a minute, and then add a king on one side of her and a queen on the other.

Chapter 21

I'M IN A RUSH to get to the auditorium after school the next day. Just as I shove my last book into my backpack, I feel a tap on my shoulder. My stomach tightens, and I take a deep breath. Slowly, I turn around. Lila is standing in front of me. Across the hall, Amelia watches us as she buttons her red peacoat.

"Hi, *Gracie*," Lila says, throwing her long, brown hair over her shoulder. I shift my eyes to Amelia, but she looks down and turns around to close her locker. *Coward!* I want to scream. "I just wanted to say hi," Lila continues, giggling. I watch her laugh. I don't know what to say.

"Well, bye, Gracie." She runs across the hall, grabs Amelia's arm, and pulls her down the hallway. Neither of them looks back, and as I watch the back of Amelia's red coat disappear, I know that she's gone.

I slam my locker shut and try to breathe evenly as I walk to the auditorium, my eyes stinging. *It's starting,* I tell myself. Aunt Sally was right.

I shove the auditorium doors open, hard, and walk over to the stage where a bunch of people are already sitting, their legs dangling over the ledge. "Hey, Grayson!" Paige calls out, as if she was waiting for me. "So, Grayson?" she goes on, and Aunt Sally's voice explodes into my head again: *He's going to get teased horribly.* I brace myself and look up at her.

"Yeah?"

"Listen, I'm sorry that I was kind of a jerk yesterday morning." I don't say anything. The room is getting quieter, and I don't check to see, but I'm sure everyone is watching us. My face is probably bright red. I *think* she's being serious.

"That's okay," I mumble. I want to look away, but I force myself to focus on her long, feathery earrings.

"No, really, it was rude. I talked . . . I mean, I thought about it last night, and I think it's really brave that you tried out for a girl's part. I'm sure you're going to make a great Persephone." She pauses. "What are you waiting for?" she finally asks. "Come on up. We leads need to stick together." She pats the stage next to her.

Her apology sounded almost rehearsed, but she's smiling now, so I make my way up the stage steps and scoot into the spot next to her. "Thanks," I say, glancing at her bright pink sweater. "So, do you know where Finn is?" I ask.

"I'm not sure," she says. "Late for our first rehearsal, I guess." She smiles at me again. I should look away. I think of Amelia. I should protect myself. But I smile back.

"There he is," Meagan says, pointing to the auditorium doors. He and Dr. Shiner are in the hallway talking, their faces just inches apart. I swallow hard and wonder if Aunt Sally actually called the school. Dr. Shiner, his face flushed, is still saying something as Finn turns and walks toward us as if nothing happened. When Dr. Shiner storms off, I glance at Paige. She shrugs and I look away.

The crowd around me has grown; everyone must be here by now. "All right, guys and gals," Finn says, taking a deep breath and walking up the steps. It looks like he's forcing himself to smile. "Sorry I'm late. Let's get started." At the back of the stage is a long table, and we turn around to face him as he sits on top of it.

"First off, congratulations! I can't tell you how excited I am about this play. We have a very impressive cast this year, and I'm confident that this performance is going to be one of the best ever."

"Woo-woo!" Paige calls out. She starts clapping, and everyone joins in.

"Thank you. Thank you very much," Finn says jokingly. "Okay. Now for logistics: the rehearsal schedule is on the bulletin board behind the stage steps. Some days only leads come, and other days everyone comes. I've already e-mailed copies of the schedule to your families."

He looks us over. "As those of you who've been in a play before know, every rehearsal we start off with a warm-up activity before turning to the script."

"That's the best part," Paige whispers to me, and I nod like I know what she's talking about.

"This week is the read-through," Finn continues. "It will take two days because we're going to discuss as we read. We want to figure out *why* these characters are doing what they're doing. So we'll warm up, and then we'll get to work. Questions so far?" He looks around at us. I want to ask him what he means by warm-up activities, but nobody else is raising their hand, so I don't, either.

"Great, then." He jumps off the table. "Let's walk the stage. Almost everyone here is a theater veteran, but for those of you who are new, I want you to feel free to observe for as long as you want to, and jump in whenever you're comfortable."

I have no idea what he's talking about, but I stand up with everyone else. I notice Finn nodding in Paige's direction, and she quickly takes my arm. "Come with me," she whispers, and guides me to an empty space at the back of the stage by the table.

"All right," Finn says over the chatter and giggles. "Everyone, quiet down and think for a minute. Who are you today? A person? An animal? A male or a female? How old are you? When you've chosen your character, start walking."

I look quickly at Paige. "Just choose someone to be," she whispers. I stare at her.

"Anyone?" I ask, starting to smile.

"Yeah. A person, an animal, anything."

She stands still for a minute, and then starts flapping her arms like they're wings. I almost start laughing. She looks completely crazy. I feel someone moving behind me and turn around to see Tommy gorilla-walking past the burgundy curtains. Meagan struts by us, her nose in the air. I feel like I'm in another world. Everyone looks completely serious and completely stupid at the same time—but stupid in a really good way.

Paige stops flapping her wings for a second and reaches over to grab my hand. I start to walk next to her. I close my eyes and try to imagine the long skirt with the amber beads swaying.

"Very nice," I hear Finn saying as we move around the stage. Paige flies off, and I keep walking. I keep imagining my skirt.

"Freeze!" Finn finally calls out, and everyone does. "Who's sharing today?"

"Oo oo, ah ah," Tommy grunts loudly, his knuckles still on the floor. He starts hopping up and down, and when Finn calls on him, he tells us that he's Tom the Gorilla and that he's super-crazed because he just escaped from the San Diego Zoo. And that his knuckles are definitely injured, and will someone please take him to the vet? I smile and clap with everyone else as Tommy stands up, shaking out his hands.

"Ouch," he says, and we all laugh.

"Great job," Finn says over our laughter. "I wish we had more time for warm-ups, but we have to get down to business. We'll walk the stage again next time." He walks over to the table.

"I'm going to pass out your scripts." We gather around him as he opens a cardboard box. "Don't lose these, please," he says, lifting a stack of red scripts out. "I don't have extras." The gold inscriptions twinkle in the overhead lights, and I hold mine carefully when Paige passes it to me.

"There are folding chairs stacked behind the curtain," Finn tells us. "Once you've gotten your script, go ahead and grab one. Carefully. I don't need an avalanche here. We're going to make a circle on the stage and start the read-through."

One by one, we inch our way behind the curtain and pull our chairs onto the stage. I stick by Paige's side, and she doesn't seem to mind. She unfolds her chair and scoots it over so I can fit in next to her. Reid pushes his chair in on the other side of me and bounces his knee up and down as he flips through his script.

"Okay," Finn says, once we're settled. "Let's start. As I said, we're going to discuss as we read." He hops up onto the table again. "Page one!"

I open my script. The spine is stiff, and the paper smells new and fresh. Tommy starts reading the prologue. "'A long time ago, in a country far away, stood Mount Olympus, the home of the Greek gods,'" he begins. "'The gods were beautiful and good, and they were not alone. Horrible creatures lived among them.

These beasts existed so gods and mortal heroes could go to war with them—so goodness and light could struggle to win.'

"'In the fields of Mount Olympus lived Persephone. She was a lovely, young girl. . . .'"

I smile to myself as he continues, but I barely pay attention to his words anymore. *She was a lovely, young girl*. The line races through me over and over again, like electricity. *A lovely, young girl.*

I look around at the cast as Tommy reads. Everyone is following along, even Finn. Meagan, Hannah, and Hailey are across from me, concentrating on their scripts. Hannah is playing absentmindedly with her long ponytail. Meagan scratches her nose. I can't believe I'm actually here. I can't believe I'm Persephone.

When Tommy finishes, Finn asks him why Hermes would want to share this story with an audience. I flip through my script as they talk. I scan my name, *Persephone*, on practically every page. *You* are *the lead,* I tell myself, smiling. I have no idea how I'm going to memorize it all.

"Grayson?" Finn calls. I look up from my script. "Earth to Grayson." He smiles. "Your line."

"Page three," Paige whispers to me, tucking her script under her thigh and reaching her hands over to help me flip back to the right page. I look up at her soft, eager face, and then over to Finn. He's still smiling, waiting patiently.

I read my monologue and, when I'm done, I look up in a daze. I glance around the auditorium. The door to the hallway is propped open now, and Dr. Shiner is leaning against the door frame. He looks like he's staring right through me, and I wonder how long he's been standing there. I look down at my fingernails quickly as Tommy reads Hermes's response to my monologue. "'Persephone had no idea what fate awaited her,'" Tommy concludes.

When I look back up, Dr. Shiner is gone.

Chapter 22

I'M HEADING TO another rehearsal, trying to make the past few days stop swirling in my head. I'm almost to the auditorium doors when I hear a voice calling my name. The hall is crowded, but right away I see Ryan and Sebastian approaching me in their identical black winter jackets.

"Hey there, Gracie," Ryan says. "You on your way to play practice?" I can't move and I glance at Sebastian, but he's looking down. "Well, I hope they have lots of pretty dresses for you to wear, freak," he says. He shoves his elbow into my side as they walk past me. I stumble a little, my eyes suddenly on fire as I turn to watch their backs disappear around the corner. I take a deep breath and try to picture myself on stage between

Paige and Reid instead of here, in the hallway, my side burning. *Ignore him,* I tell myself, and I walk to the auditorium. *Always ignore him.*

It started the other day after Humanities. When the bell rang and I got up to leave, I saw him staring at me. Finn was across the room, digging through a cabinet. I headed for the door, but Ryan got up and stepped in front of me. I walked around him, tucking my long bangs behind my ears. "You letting your hair grow out, Gracie?" he asked, watching me go.

The next day, he and Sebastian appeared silently at my desk before Finn came in. Ryan had a fake-sweet look on his face. I looked away and watched the door. Where was Finn? "I'm not trying to be rude, Grayson," Ryan said, even though I wouldn't look at him. "We're just wondering—I mean, *everyone's* wondering—why are you playing a girl? Are you gay or something?" The room shook, like the first rumblings of an earthquake. I looked at Sebastian. I don't know why. Maybe to see if he felt it, too, but he was looking out the window. A minute later, Finn walked in and shooed everyone to their seats.

I push open the doors to the auditorium. Hard, to shake these memories out of my head. Today is practice for leads only, and Tommy, Reid, Audrey, and Natalie are sitting together on the ledge of the stage, talking to Finn. They wave to me as I walk toward them. "Hey, Grayson!" they all call out together. Then they look at each other, surprised to hear their voices in unison, and collapse practically on top of one another, laughing.

I feel my body relaxing as I join them. Paige isn't here yet, so I sit down next to Reid, who's still hysterical. The auditorium doors bang open. Paige and Meagan walk in together and toss their backpacks onto the wooden seats. Finn looks at his watch. "We'll give it a few more minutes. We're just waiting for Andrew, right?"

"He's coming," Paige says. "I saw him at his locker. He was totally freaking out because he couldn't find his English binder. Have you ever seen his locker?" she asks us. I smile at her when her eyes meet mine. "It's beyond disgusting. I think he has old lunches in there from, like, September." She climbs the stage steps and sits down right next to me. Meagan follows her. I glance at the other empty spaces where she could have sat instead, and I smile.

"Hey," I say to her.

"Hey, yourself," she replies. "So, Finn?" she asks, suddenly turning to him. "Have you been to the Shakespeare Theater?"

"Of course! I was just there last week," he answers. "Why do you ask?"

"My dad got us tickets to *Romeo and Juliet*," she says. "Is that what you saw?"

"It was," he answers. "Opening night."

"Did you like it? I've heard it's *amazing*."

"It *was* amazing," Finn answers. "We'll discuss it, but *after* you see it. I can't wait to hear what you think!"

"Cool," Paige says.

I watch them talking. Reid is on one side of me, and Paige

is on the other. They're like bookends, and I concentrate on the feel of their arms on either side of me as we wait for Andrew.

When he finally slams through the door, apologizing, we take our places for Act One. Tommy has his entire monologue memorized, and, when it's time for me and Paige to go onstage, she leaves her script on top of her backpack in the chair next to Finn. I wonder again how I'm going to memorize everything. "Ready?" I ask Finn from the stage, my script in hand.

"Whenever you guys are," he calls up to us.

I turn to the right page. "'Mother,'" I call, and it feels so weird to say it out loud. I try to not smile and to stay in character, like Finn told us to. Paige is pulling pretend weeds in the corner of the stage. "'I'm going to the stream,'" I tell her.

"'Be careful, Persephone,'" she says.

"'Yes, Mother.'" I look down at my script. It's her line, but she's looking at me expectantly. *"What time will you be back?"* I whisper to her.

My line? she mouths, surprised. I nod, and she almost starts laughing.

"'What time will you be back?'"

"'Before dark,'" I read. The stage is quiet. *"Persephone, I'd like you to bring some of the Elves along,"* I whisper. I burst out laughing. I can't help it. Obviously, she doesn't have her part memorized as well as she thinks. I take a deep breath and try to compose myself.

"'Persephone, I'd like you to bring some of the Elves along,'" Paige repeats. Suddenly, a red script sails through the air, like a

Frisbee, and lands at Paige's feet. We both look out at the auditorium, hysterical now. Finn waves at us from the front row of seats.

"Maybe we'll take our snack break early today?" he asks. I can't stop laughing as I dig my brown paper bag out of my backpack.

☆

At home, I eat dinner quickly. I want to get to my room so I can finish my math homework and memorize lines. I don't have too many problems left—I've been getting so much done in the library at lunchtime. "You're on a *mission*," Mrs. Millen said to me earlier today as she sat at her desk with her steaming lunch and Diet Coke and watched me fly through my assignments. It's true. I want to be able to focus on memorizing lines once I'm home. "Getting into Persephone's skin," as Finn puts it, is the best part of my day.

And anyway, I don't want to be around Aunt Sally. I look up from my food. She's watching me eat, and I look out the window at the black sky. I heard what she said. She thinks I'm a monster.

"So, Grayson," Jack says, as he shoves rice into his mouth, "do you know what Tyler asked me in gym today?" I freeze. Jack's new best friend, Tyler, is Ryan's older brother.

"No," I mumble.

"He asked me if being gay is genetic."

I accidentally drop my fork onto my plate.

"Jack! We're not getting into this with you again," Uncle Evan warns.

"Whatever," Jack mumbles. "Of course you're not. It's all about what *Grayson* wants. That's how it's always been. You don't even care about me." I can't believe he could possibly think that.

"Don't be ridiculous," Aunt Sally says quickly.

"Why don't you just try ignoring Tyler?" Brett asks. "At school, Mr. Smith always says if you have a conflict with someone, you can try ignoring them."

"Shut up, Brett," Jack says.

"Why? Anyway, I still don't get it. I mean, it's just a play."

I can't listen anymore. "I'm finished," I say as I get up from the table. "I have to work on my lines."

In my room, I sit on my bed under Mom's painting with my script in my lap. I've got to get this memorized by rehearsal tomorrow, but it's hard to concentrate. Jack's words echo in my ears. I can't believe how stupid he is.

There's a gentle knock on the door, and Uncle Evan comes in. He sits at my desk. "So," he says softly, "you have a lot to do?"

"Yeah," I tell him. "Everyone's starting to get their lines memorized but me."

"You know," he says, "when I was in law school, I had to figure out how to remember thousands of pages of information."

"You did?"

"Sure. It was pretty intense. What I would do is try to visualize the pages in my mind, you know? Like, I'd read a section of information, and then close my eyes and try to actually see some of the key words. It really helped." He pauses. "You want to try that? I could help you—you know, read along to see if you're getting it?"

I look at him. Dad looks so young in the pictures that we have of him, and I wonder: if he were alive, would he and Uncle Evan still look alike? Would his hair be turning gray above the ears, too? Would he push his glasses up with his knuckle when they slipped down on his nose? I hear dishes clanging in the kitchen, and the TV is on now. Uncle Evan gets up and quietly closes my door all the way.

"Sure," I tell him, and hand him my script.

"So, Act One, huh?" he asks, scanning the words.

"Yeah."

"Great. Whenever you're ready, Grayson."

"Uncle Evan?"

"Yes, son?" he asks, without looking up.

The words are like a slap, but I try to ignore the feeling. "Thanks," I say.

"My pleasure." He looks up and smiles at me. "Your line."

Chapter 23

THE AUDITORIUM IS CHAOTIC. I'd forgotten that the whole cast, including all the Elves and Souls of the Underworld, would be at rehearsal today. Reid, Andrew, and Tommy are on the stage with a couple other boys. They're talking, and then laughing too loudly at something one of them is saying.

The girls are in the front rows of auditorium seats. Paige is already there, and, of course, she's in the middle of the group. Hailey, Hannah, and a bunch of the Elves are gathered around her. Natalie and Audrey walk in together. They say hi to me on their way to the front of the auditorium. A few more people hurry past, but I hang back.

Finally, Meagan walks in. "You coming, Grayson?" she asks.

I glance at the boys onstage again, their movements quick and their voices booming.

"Yeah, I'm coming," I say, and I follow her to the wooden seats.

I keep my eyes fixed on Paige, who smiles when she sees me. "Hey, Grayson!" she calls. Everyone looks up at me, and I let my eyes scan their faces for a second. "Come sit with me," she says, moving her jacket and backpack off of the seat next to her. I wonder if she saved it for me.

I scoot past Sofia, one of the Elves. Hannah is leaning over her, holding a tiny pink clip between her lips and making a thin braid down the side of her head. Her fingers move quickly, like they know what they're doing, and when she's done she clasps the braid at the bottom.

"'Kay," Hannah says, "who's next?" I notice that she has a pack of tiny clips resting on top of her pink backpack. They're arranged in the package like a rainbow—pink, peach, yellow, light green, light blue, and lavender, the colors lined up in neat plastic rows.

"Me!" says Meagan from the row in front of her.

"Color?" asks Hannah. I watch them talk. Their voices crisscross easily, back and forth, and the rhythm of their words reminds me of "Miss Mary Mack, Mack, Mack" and "Bo Bo Ski Watten Totten" and all the years of recesses I spent sitting on the cement step outside with a book in my hands, pretending to read, but really watching the girls. Wishing.

"Um, do two next to each other. Blue and purple."

"Lean over," Hannah says, and Meagan does.

I watch Hannah's hands fly until two perfect, long, black braids appear on the side of Meagan's head. I reach up, run my fingers through my longish hair, and I look over at Paige. She's glancing at her watch. "It's already almost three twenty-five. Where's Finn?" she asks, to nobody in particular. He's come in late almost every day.

"Here he is," someone says, and I look up to see him jogging down the auditorium aisle.

"Afternoon, ladies," he says, nodding in our direction, and I glance at the other girls quickly. I doubt he noticed me huddled in the middle of the group, but Sofia giggles.

"Shh," Paige says.

"Gentlemen," Finn nods to the boys on the stage. "Sorry I'm late. I'd like everyone to join the boys up here," he continues. "I need you all to grab a mat from this pile and find your own space on the stage. We're doing something new for warm-up." He points to a stack of yoga mats that someone must have brought in from the gym. The mob of girls surrounding me starts to move, and I'm part of the clump. We walk together onto the stage. "It's going to be kind of tight with all of you here. Spread out as much as you can! Lie down on a mat on your back," Finn calls up to us. "We're doing a relaxation exercise!"

I unroll a mat and smile to myself when Paige puts hers right next to mine. She lies down and closes her eyes. I lie next to her. Above me, the ceiling looks like it's about a million miles away. The stage lights are bright, so I close my eyes, too. The mat smells gross, and I hear people walking and talking above me. When the stage finally starts to quiet down, I look to my right and see that Andrew is next to me now, too.

"I could fall asleep," he whispers.

"Definitely." I smile.

"Okay," Finn finally says quietly from somewhere on the stage. "Today we're going to start building some relaxation exercises into our rehearsal routine. Many actors use relaxation and visualization techniques to help them settle into their characters. We're going to start by relaxing each muscle group in our bodies, one by one. We'll begin with our toes and work our way up to our necks."

I listen to Finn's voice. He tells us to tighten our muscles, and then feel them relax. By the time he has gotten to our necks, the room is completely silent.

He's practically whispering to us now. "Now that you're relaxed, we're going to begin our visualization exercises. Keep your eyes closed. Picture yourself on stage rehearsing. You are no longer yourself—you *are* your character." He pauses, and then continues, even slower. "How do you want to see yourself?" he asks us. "Look down and imagine your body, your clothes. What do you see?" He pauses. The quiet is long and still. "What, as a character, do you need to learn, and what do you already know? Think about this. Make a mental list." He waits, the silence hanging over the stage, heavy now. I can practically feel it seeping into the open spaces around me. "What are you afraid of?" Another long pause. "And, finally, what do you wish for?"

My muscles suddenly tighten. I open my eyes and stare at the track of lights dangling far above my head. My heart is racing, and I try to focus on the pattern—black, light, black, light, black, light, but the light is seeping into the black spaces and everything is too bright to look at for so long. I close my eyes again, but I'm still blinded by the bursts of light floating in front of me. I feel dizzy, like I'm spinning, and I'm starting to feel like a bird again, like I did that day in Humanities so long ago when Amelia asked me to be her partner.

The auditorium is silent, but Finn's voice echoes in my head. *What do you wish for?* I'm flying above myself now, looking down at the stage that's slowly swirling beneath me. I'm like the phoenix in Mom's painting. All the colors beneath me are blending together. Paige and Andrew are on either side of me. Their eyes are closed. My eyes are open. I'm clutching the sides of my yoga mat.

What are you afraid of? I hear Aunt Sally's voice ripping through my head again: *He's creating a monster!* But I don't look like a monster. I look the way I'm *supposed* to look—the way I need everyone else to see me. I'm wearing the long, lacy skirt with dangling amber beads. It's like an antique. It's something Persephone would wear. My blond hair is a fan around my face. I look scared, but also pretty. My heartbeat surrounds me like the drumbeat that I heard at tryouts. I remember it now—how it felt when I first knew that I was supposed to be Persephone.

What do you already know?

I am a girl.

Part Three

Chapter 24

AUNT SALLY'S HAIR *is blond like mine. I wonder if she wore it in braids when she was a girl.* This is what I'm thinking, and I don't know why, as I feel the gentle *tug tug tug* on my head. I imagine Paige's fingers crisscrossing quickly, like they know what they're doing. "Pass me a clip," she says to Meagan. It's Tuesday after school, leads only, and when Paige said she'd make me a braid, I shrugged and smiled.

I feel one last *tug*, and warm plastic against my cheekbone. "Cute," Paige says, and smiles. It's like she can read my mind, because she adds, "I'll make you another one." She gathers my hair at my scalp, and the gentle tugging starts again. When she's done, I can hear the two plastic clips clanking together. I see the pink and purple out of the corner of my eye when I turn my face.

"You look fabulous, Grayson," Natalie says, grinning. I can't tell if she's kidding or not, but either way, her face looks kind, so I smile back.

Finn won't be in for a few more minutes even though rehearsal is supposed to start at three fifteen. I reach up to touch the bumpy braids and plastic clips.

"So, Meagan," Paige suddenly asks, "what's up with you and Sebastian?"

"Oh my God," Meagan says, rolling her eyes. "Why does everyone keep asking me that?" She sounds annoyed, but I can tell she's trying not to smile. "Who told you?"

"Um, Liam?" Liam is Sebastian's older brother. I follow the conversation carefully with my eyes, trying not to seem too interested or shocked, but I can't believe what Meagan is saying. Sebastian? Ryan's loser sidekick? What is she thinking? A thought wrestles its way into my mind—have Meagan and Sebastian ever talked about *me*?

"So, what's going on?" Paige nudges. "Are you guys together or something?"

"I don't know!" Meagan squeals.

"Well, I think he's cute," Paige says, just as Finn slams through the auditorium doors.

"Sorry," he yells. "Sorry I'm late."

"As usual," Audrey mumbles under her breath, and the girls stand up to move onto the stage for relaxation.

I stay where I am for a minute and reach up to touch the two plastic clips hanging next to my cheek. Meagan's long, black hair swings as she walks toward the aisle.

Andrew, Reid, and Tommy are already on the stage, laying out their mats, and Finn is talking to them. The four of them are laughing. I pull the clips off the ends of my braids, tuck them into my pocket, and run my fingers through my hair. I feel the braids unravel as I join the others onstage.

☆

On Friday Paige is absent, and I stand in the aisle for a minute, studying the growing group of girls in the auditorium seats. Meagan is in the middle of the clump. Hannah and Hailey are on one side of her, and Audrey and Natalie are on the other. They're bunched together, talking. I walk over to them and sit down in front of Meagan. I feel lost without Paige, and I open my backpack to take out a book to pretend to read.

"Hey, Grayson," Meagan says, so I turn around. I've been watching her and Sebastian this past week, and if they really are together, they spend a lot of time ignoring each other.

"Grayson, lean over," Natalie says, and I see she has a handful of clips. "Let's braid your hair again."

"Okay." I smile, put my book back into my backpack, and turn around on my knees to face the girls behind me. She reaches for my hair, and I feel her fingers gently scratch my scalp.

"Um, are you braiding Grayson's hair?" a sixth grader named Kristen asks from behind me. She's one of the Elves.

"Yeah, he looks fab with braids," Natalie says as she works, and I glance back at Kristen while Natalie hangs onto a clump of my hair.

"Okaaay," Kristen says. I can't tell what she's thinking.

Nobody says anything for a minute. Finally, Kristen asks, "Want some help?" and I see Audrey pass her some clips.

Kaylee is sitting next to me now. "Can I have a few?" she asks, laughter in her voice. I look at her out of the corner of my eye as Natalie tugs at my hair, and soon a million hands are flying over my head. Someone's pulling too hard. I don't know who, but I don't say anything. I reach my hand up to feel what's going on, but Natalie tells me to wait, so I do.

Meagan gives me a thumbs-up as Natalie, Kristen, and Kaylee work, and I notice that Hannah and Audrey are both talking to her at the same time. She's looking back and forth between them, like she's stuck in the middle of two worlds, and for some reason, this makes me smile.

By the time Finn comes in, the girls are done. I reach my hands up and feel my head. It's completely covered in braids and clips and, all of a sudden, I feel almost guilty—like I just cheated on a test and didn't get caught. But I push that thought away. "So? What do you think?" I ask, turning my head from side to side. I know I must look like a clown, but everyone's smiling at me now, so I don't really care.

"Super adorable," Natalie says, and we walk up to the stage. Finn smiles at me as I take my yoga mat off the pile. It's kind of uncomfortable to lie on top of a million clips during relaxation, but I leave them in anyway.

☆

When rehearsal is over, I stand in the aisle pulling clips out of my hair and unraveling my braids. I watch everyone zip themselves into their winter jackets and put on their backpacks as I work.

"Need some help?" Meagan asks from behind me. I turn around. She's standing with Hannah and Hailey. They look like an ad for the Gap in their pink and purple shiny jackets, their hair smooth and long.

"Nah, I'm almost done," I say. I think of the girls' voices and grins as I let them braid my hair, and the feeling washes over me again—that I did something wrong and got away with it. I let them treat me like I was a stupid doll or something. Anyway, what *real* girl wears a million crooked braids all over her head, sticking out all over the place? *Real girls* wear regular shirts, pants, skirts, jackets, and shoes, not crazy, exaggerated porcupine braids that make them look like an idiot. This was all just a big joke to everyone. I pass Hannah my handful of clips, and she zips them into the outside pocket of her pink backpack. I suddenly feel like crying, and I pat my head to make sure I got them all out.

"I think you're good," Meagan says, examining my hair. "Ready to go?"

"Yeah," I say. I swing my gray backpack onto my back and tuck my jacket under my arm.

"You taking the bus home?" Meagan asks as we walk out the auditorium doors.

"No, my uncle's picking me up on his way home from work," I tell her. "You?"

"My mom's getting us."

"Cool."

"So, do you still go to the library at lunch?" she asks.

I look down at my shoes. "Yeah, I try to get my homework done so I can memorize lines at night. My uncle's been helping me." I run my fingers through my hair one more time.

"Well, if you ever want to eat with us, you should," she says as we approach the double doors to the parking lot.

I look at Meagan and smile. Hannah and Hailey are standing on either side of her, watching her. "Thanks, Meagan," I tell her. And I mean it, but I know I'll never be able to sit at the same table as Lila and Amelia again.

Outside at the circle drive, Meagan's mom is waiting in a silver SUV. "Bye, Grayson," the girls say, and they pile into the car, one shining jacket at a time—first pink, then purple, then pink again. Meagan's mom rolls down the passenger window and leans toward me.

"Hi, Grayson!" she calls, and I suddenly feel panicky. I'm sure she knows I'm Persephone. "Are you getting picked up?"

"Yeah, my uncle should be here any minute."

"Okay, as long as you have a ride. Have a good weekend!"

I stand in the cold, damp air and wait for Uncle Evan. I should put my jacket on, but I don't want to. I look at it, hanging over my arm—dull and black—and I try to picture what I wish were there instead. *Real girls wear regular shirts, pants, skirts, jackets, and shoes.* I think about the braids again. I don't want to look like a freak. I want to be a real girl.

Uncle Evan pulls up, and I get into the car. The heat is blasting, and the news is on the radio. "Hey, Grayson," he says as I buckle my seat belt. "How's everything?"

"Good," I tell him.

"Great. So listen, I hate to say this, but I'm not going to be able to practice lines with you tomorrow morning. Sorry about that. Something came up at work, and I need to go in to meet with Henry." He looks distracted. "We'll definitely do it Sunday, though, okay?"

"That's fine. It's not a problem." I almost feel relieved. *Real girls wear regular shirts, pants, skirts, jackets, and shoes.* "Actually, I was thinking of going to that thrift store in Lake View tomorrow, anyway. Is that okay?" The words tumble out of my mouth.

Uncle Evan looks at me quickly. "You going with Amelia?"

"Nope," I say. "No. Just me."

"Sure. I'm sure that's fine," he says as he pulls onto the street.

Chapter 25

THE NEXT MORNING, it looks slushy and gray out. I crack my window open. It's way too warm for the end of January, and the wet air floats into my room, through the screen. I get dressed in my jeans and a sweatshirt, and grab my light blue fleece from my closet.

It feels strange to be riding the bus alone to the Second Hand. I haven't done this since last summer, since before Amelia. The bus bumps and bounces through potholes as I watch out the steamy window.

In Lake View, the crowd feels familiar as I make my way down the sidewalk. I don't look up as I pass the floor-to-ceiling window at the Coffee House, but a shudder zips through my body anyway. The wind is blowing like crazy behind me, and it practically pushes me through the doorway of the Second Hand.

Inside, everything is the same. It's dreary and dim and smells like mothballs. I pass the shelves of knickknacks. I want to look, to see if the broken bird is still there lying at the bottom of its cage, but I don't. I doubt it, anyway. I walk to the empty youth section.

I glance at the racks of boys' clothes, and I remember all the time I spent sifting through them, looking for things that I could easily pretend into dresses and long, flowing shirts, and, for a tiny second, I miss doing that. It seems so safe. But, on the other side of the room are the racks of girls' clothes, and I go to them.

I look behind me at the guy at the register with the shaved head, and at the few people shopping in the front of the store. *It's my sister's birthday this week,* I silently rehearse. *She asked for clothes for a present.* I look through the racks of T-shirts hanging on the wall and pull out a pink one with a sequined heart on it. It looks like it will fit me. I want to browse slowly, to feel the fabric of each T-shirt on the rack; I want to try them on, but I tell myself to hurry. I quickly find two others that I like, a lavender one with a light ruffle of lace around the bottom, and a fuchsia one with colorful butterflies embroidered on the sleeves. I take a deep breath and walk with them to the register. *It's my sister's birthday this week. She asked for clothes for a present.*

There's someone in line ahead of me, so I drape the shirts over my arm and run my fingers through a bowl of silver rings on the front counter. One looks like a braid, and I try it on. It makes me think of Paige. Next to the rings, necklaces dangle from a metal stand. I examine them—the crosses, hearts, and colorful beads, and I look carefully at a bird charm hanging from a silver chain. Its wings are spread; it's mid-flight. I turn the tag over. Ten dollars.

"You all set?" I look up. It's my turn.

"Um, yeah." My hands kind of shake as I put the shirts on the counter. I put the necklace on top of them. The guy pulls out the tag on each shirt. He doesn't look up, and it crosses my mind for a quick second that maybe he wouldn't care that the clothes are for me.

"You find everything okay?" he asks.

"Yeah."

"Cool," he says, finally looking at me. He smiles.

"It's, uh, it's my sister's birthday this week," I stammer. "She wanted clothes for her present."

"This is a cool necklace," he says as he rings it up.

"Yeah."

"Twenty-four eighteen," he says, putting everything into a plastic bag.

I hand him twenty-five dollars and wait for my change. "Hope your sister has a good birthday," he says, handing it to me. I put the coins into my pocket, grab the bag, and head out the door.

Chapter 26

THE REST OF the weekend crawls by. When Monday morning finally comes, I wake up early in my dim room and put on my jeans. I take the plastic bag out from where I hid it behind the summer clothes in my closet, pull out the necklace and pink shirt with the sparkly heart, and carefully snap off both tags. I crumple them up and throw them in my garbage can before tucking the bag back behind my shorts.

Standing in front of my mirror, I watch myself pull my pajama shirt off and put on the T-shirt. The heart lies flat on my chest. I clasp the necklace behind my neck, brush my hair and tuck it behind my ears, and stand there for a long time, looking at myself. I wonder what Paige would think.

When I hear the shower running across the hall, though,

panic gushes through me. I open the other side of my closet, pull out my dark purple hoodie, put it on quickly, and zip it up all the way to the top. I look like my old self in it, but still, I can't help smiling as I wait for my turn in the bathroom.

☆

At school, Finn is late to Humanities again. I pretend to be looking for something in my backpack so I don't have to make eye contact with anyone. I pay attention to the feel of the T-shirt underneath my hoodie while I wait for him to come in.

When the bell finally rings, I look to the door. Still no Finn, but Ryan is making his way to my desk now. I touch my hand to the top of my zipper and look back down to my backpack.

"Hey—*Grace*!" Ryan whispers. I keep my head down. *"Gracie!"*

And then, Finn's voice. "All right, class! Sorry I'm late. Everyone, take your seat. Ryan? In your seat please." I take deep breaths. "Notebooks open!" Finn picks up a dry-erase marker. "Everybody's copy of *To Kill a Mockingbird* should be out. Let's get started." I press my fingers to the bird flying under my sweatshirt as I listen to him talk.

☆

When Science is finally over at three o'clock, I lean down to pack my backpack. Meagan and Hannah are lab partners right behind me, and when I stand up, I see Sebastian walking toward them with a little smile on his face. His hands are in his pockets. "Hi, Meagan," he says shyly. I look back and forth between their faces.

"Sebastian!" I hear from across the room, and I turn around. Ryan is pushing his way toward us, through everyone who's heading for the door. "Watch it," he says to Sofia as he shoves past her. "Sebastian, let's go. My mom always picks me up out front." I head for the door and glance behind me one more time as I pass Mrs. Leo's desk. Sebastian is saying something to Ryan. His face is flushed.

Suddenly, I hear Mrs. Leo's voice. "Grayson, do you have a moment?" I look over to her. She's always asking people to stay behind to help her clean lab supplies.

"Oh, sorry, I have to get to rehearsal," I call from the doorway.

"Oh, that's right. Well, it will only take five minutes or so. Don't after-school activities start at three fifteen? I wanted to talk to you and Sebastian for a minute."

My heart jumps. Why?

I glance up at the clock on the wall. "Okay." I head back to her desk.

"Sebastian?" she calls across the room. He looks over and his eyes widen.

"Yeah?" he asks.

"I need to talk to you and Grayson for a moment." Ryan looks at Sebastian and smirks. Then he covers his mouth with his hands and fake-gags. Mrs. Leo seems totally oblivious.

“’Kay,” Sebastian mumbles, and Ryan, Meagan, and Hannah head out the door. Sebastian joins me in front of Mrs. Leo’s desk. She takes her glasses off and pushes them up onto her white curls.

“So, boys,” she starts, and I feel like she just punched me in the face with her tiny, knotted, veiny fist. I look down at my shoes. “You know, I’ve been a teacher here at Porter for almost forty years.”

I nod and swallow, and glance over to Sebastian. What does she want?

“Well,” she continues, “in all my years here I’ve never . . .” She pauses and looks almost embarrassed. I glance down to make sure my zipper on my sweatshirt is still up. My heart is pounding in my ears.

“Well, I’ve never been able to get enough kids together who are interested in starting a Science Club.”

My breathing evens, and I feel my body relaxing. I look at Sebastian. He seems relieved, too.

Her face lights up. “So, you fellows are interested?” she asks quickly. “I’m looking for a few kids from every grade to head it up—good students who have a solid understanding of science.”

I speak up first. “Um, sorry, Mrs. Leo. I can’t. I’m too busy with rehearsal.” I glance at Sebastian, and then over to the clock on the wall again.

“Yeah,” he mumbles. “I, um, I have guitar after school. And homework.” His voice trails off, and I smile to myself as I listen to him trying to come up with an excuse.

"Oh, okay," Mrs. Leo says, disappointed. "You kids are all so busy these days."

I inch backward to the door. "Sorry about that, Mrs. Leo," I say. "If I change my mind, I'll let you know," I tell her, my hand on the doorknob. I need to get to rehearsal.

Sebastian is by my side. "Yeah, sorry," he says awkwardly.

The hallways are emptying out as we walk to our lockers downstairs. I glance over at Sebastian. I picture him at Ryan's side, but then I think of the way he smiled at Meagan after class today. "That was close," I say.

He keeps his eyes on the floor. "Yup." He's quiet for a minute before he looks at me and smiles. "Seriously."

At my locker, I grab my books and jacket and shove everything into my backpack. Sebastian shuts his locker across the hall from me, and when I start to walk toward the auditorium, he's by my side again.

I touch my bird charm through my sweatshirt as we turn the corner away from the main hallway. The hall outside of the auditorium is almost empty. It looks like everyone is either at their after-school activity by now or has left the building, except for Sebastian and me and a couple of kids down by the front doors.

When we get closer to the auditorium, though, I stop walking. I see now that the two figures at the far end of the hallway are Ryan and Tyler. For the billionth time, I think about Aunt Sally's prediction, and I turn to look at Sebastian. He's watching them, too. They're coming toward us, and I can see the smirks on their stupid faces. And even though a little piece of me still hopes they're just here to meet Sebastian, the truth is that I know they're not. I know they're here for me.

The four of us are so close to each other now. Tyler is bigger than Ryan, but aside from that, they look almost identical with their straight bangs and hard faces.

"Hey, Sebastian," Ryan says once we're face-to-face. But he's looking at me. "Mrs. Leo didn't want to make you and Gracie lab partners, did she? 'Cause who would I be with, then?" Sebastian is looking toward the doors at the end of the hallway. He shakes his head no.

I keep my fingers on my zipper. "So, Gracie-girl," Ryan continues, "why were you ignoring me in Humanities today?"

I don't say anything. My mouth won't work.

"Grace," Tyler pipes in. "Why won't you just talk to us? Jack told me if we wanted to talk to you, we could find you here after school. So why aren't you talking to us?"

I feel like I'm in a cloud. Sebastian takes a few steps back until he's leaning against the lockers. "I've gotta go," I say to Ryan and Tyler. The words spill out. I don't even feel myself talking. My hand is still holding my zipper. But Ryan takes a step closer, blocking me.

"You going to the auditorium to play dress-up?" he asks as Tyler comes to his side. "I bet they have lots of pretty things for you to wear." He glances up at his brother and smiles.

My mouth opens and closes. I'm dizzy. I hold tight to my zipper.

"Hey, look, Ry," Tyler says, pointing to my hand on my zipper.

"You're right. He's all ready to put his dress on." He turns back to me. "Why are you such a freak?" he asks.

I can't get my hand to move. He takes a step closer and grabs my sweatshirt. I stumble forward into him. He smells like sweat. I look over to Sebastian again, but he's standing with his arms hanging limply at his sides.

Suddenly, I hear shouting behind me. Ryan and Tyler look over my shoulder, and I turn around. Paige is rushing toward us, her backpack thumping against her side. "Hey! Hey! What's going on?" she yells, and in a second, she's by my side. She wraps her arm around mine.

Ryan and Tyler don't say anything. "Well," Tyler finally says, "we were just talking to Gracie." He smiles at Paige. Her face turns bright pink, and I can practically feel the heat rising from her body. I lean into her a little.

"Why don't you just get away from him?" she yells, even though they're standing right in front of us.

"Whoa, calm down, psycho," Tyler whispers. He glances around the hallway, and he and Ryan start to back away. I look at Sebastian. He's watching Paige, and he looks relieved.

"That's right," Paige continues. "Just get away from us, you coward idiots. Run on home. Losers!"

I stare at her. I don't know what to say. I can't believe the words flying out of her mouth. Ryan and Tyler look around nervously. "Come on, Ry," Tyler finally says. "We've gotta go anyway. Dad's picking us up at the west door."

"I thought it was Mom's week," Ryan stumbles.

"Well, you thought wrong," Tyler says, and grabs him by the arm. They turn and run off, banging through the side doors of the school, and are gone. The hallway is silent except for my breathing and the sound of the blood racing through my veins. Sebastian hasn't moved.

The auditorium doors suddenly slam open, and Finn barges through. "Paige!" he yells from down the hallway. "What on earth is going on?"

I grab her hand and look her in the eye. "Don't tell," I demand. I don't know why I say it.

"Are you insane?" she whispers.

"I'm serious," I say. "Please."

"Why?" she asks as Finn walks toward us. A crowd of heads is poking out of the auditorium door behind him now.

"I . . . I don't know," I say. And I don't. I feel dangerously close to a cliff. "Just, please?"

She looks at me like I'm crazy. "Okay," she says. I don't want to let go of her arm, but Finn is standing over us now.

"What is this screaming about?" he asks. "Is everything okay?"

"Yeah," Paige answers, looking him in the eye. "Sorry, Finn."

"All right, then," he says, studying us as we stand there, side by side. His eyes rest on mine for what seems like forever. *You sure?* they beg.

I'm sure. I drop Paige's arm and shove my fists into my pockets.

Finn still doesn't move. "Grayson, you know if you ever need to tell me anything, you can, right?" he asks.

"I know," I mumble. I can't say anything else.

We stand together in silence. "All right, then," he finally says again. "We should get to the auditorium."

I glance back as we follow him down the hall. Sebastian is gone.

Chapter 27

EVERYTHING KEEPS flip-flopping back and forth, from bad to good, over and over again. Sometimes everything is light. Other times, everything is dark.

In class, and with Aunt Sally and Jack at home, I keep my head down and my fingers on the zipper at my neck. During these times, I want to become invisible again, the way I used to be.

But at rehearsal, it's totally different.

I'm sitting with the other leads, our feet dangling off the stage. I look up at the stage lights hanging above us and at the spaces between them—the blackness fading into light over and over again. Paige is on one side of me, and Andrew is on the other. "Ladies and gentlemen!" Finn is saying. "I never thought that by February we'd be so far along. This is going to be a very, very strong performance!" I picture myself as Persephone, onstage in the dark, crowded auditorium, and I smile.

"Last time, we were talking about Act Three," Finn goes on, and Reid raises his hand to ask him something about the scenery in the Underworld. I can picture myself sitting on Hades's bench in my golden gown.

"Hey, what's so funny?" Andrew whispers, nudging me playfully.

"Huh?" I ask, looking up at him. He starts to giggle. I must have been staring into space, smiling. "Nah, nothing," I grin. I know if I keep looking at him, I'm going to burst out laughing, so I look down at my feet.

All of our shoes are hanging over the stage ledge, and the trip that Aunt Sally and Uncle Evan took us on to the Grand Canyon two summers ago pops into my head. I remember standing at the edge of the cliff, looking over the railing, and feeling so close to falling. Once, when we were hiking, I tripped on a rock and stumbled toward the edge of the path that dropped off into a steep, rocky hill. It was Jack who reached out his hand to grab mine.

I listen to Finn's voice as he continues to talk, but I can't hear his words anymore. The feeling of the crystal light fades into blackness as I envision myself, onstage, as Persephone again. Now I feel like I'm a step away from that cliff.

I automatically check the zipper on my sweatshirt to make sure that it's up all the way. I try to clear my mind and focus on Finn's words: "If there aren't any questions, we'll jump right in!"

Everyone scrambles for their places. I push the memory of the cliff out of my mind as I walk to center stage. The Souls of the Underworld are wandering the stage, watching me. They're waiting for me to give my line. Uncle Evan and I practiced this scene last night, and I know it perfectly.

I sit down on the bench next to Kristen and watch the deathly Souls as they roam around us. Everything is damp and dreary. "'I'm so lonely in the Underworld,'" I say to Kristen, and I try to describe the *feeling* of happiness up above, but I can't put it into words. I forget about the evil in her eyes. I'm daydreaming, thinking of my mother in her garden, and, distracted, I reach for a pomegranate from the cardboard tree next to us. I break it open with my thumbs and put a seed into my mouth, not noticing Kristen's slight smile.

Finn interrupts just as Zeus and Hades are coming into the garden to find me. By then, I've eaten six pomegranate seeds. "Listen up for a minute here," Finn says. "I want you to notice how well Grayson has gotten into character. Well done, Grayson." Everyone looks at me and I can't help smiling, even though I try to tighten my lips. "That was golden," Finn goes on. "Golden."

Across the stage, Paige is nodding, like she agrees with him. She catches me looking at her, flashes a smile, and gives me a thumbs-up.

☆

When I get home after rehearsal, Jack and Brett are already there. An open cereal box and two dirty bowls are on the dining room table, and I can hear their voices from across the apartment. On the way to my bedroom, I pass Jack's closed door. His Nerf ball thumps against it, and he and Brett suddenly burst into laughter. I swallow hard. I know they're on Jack's bed shooting baskets from across the room. Someone jumps onto the rug and scrambles for the ball.

I quietly close my bedroom door against the sounds and take out my math book. Uncle Evan promised me we'd practice lines after dinner again and I want to be ready, but it's hard to concentrate. Even with my door closed, I can hear them jumping and laughing, and I remember when Jack and I used to play this same game together, bare feet on messy blankets, the orange Nerf ball soft in our hands.

The weeks pass by. It's bitter cold out now. I spend every second that I'm not at rehearsal or practicing my lines wishing that I were. One Friday, after Paige meets me at my locker and walks me to the auditorium like she always does, Finn comes in with a small cardboard box in his hands. The other girls and I join the boys on the stage. I notice that Dr. Shiner is taking a seat in the back row. He must have walked in a step behind Finn.

Finn stands in front of us with a wide smile on his face.

"We're about a month away from the big day!" he tells us. "I got you all something. Thankfully, we came in just under budget, so . . ." He opens the box, takes out a brightly colored rubber bracelet, and holds it up. It's red, yellow, and blue swirled together—primary colors. "Just a little symbol of our solidarity. It says *The Myth of Persephone* on it," he announces proudly, putting it on his wrist. He holds his arm up for everyone to see.

"Cool," Paige whispers next to me.

Finn hands the box to Kaylee. She takes a bracelet and passes the box down. When it comes to me, I take one out, pull it onto my wrist, and look at the slanted inscription: *The Myth of Persephone*.

"Definitely cool," I say to Paige. She holds her wrist up in front of me.

"Cheers!" she says, smiling. We clink bracelets.

For a second, I think about how perfect it would be if I could freeze time. I'd stay right here forever.

But obviously, that's impossible.

At home that night, I change into my pajamas and bring my three dirty T-shirts across the hall to the bathroom with the small baggie of Woolite I took from the laundry room. My fingers become red and numb as I knead the shirts in the icy water in the sink. I can feel the bracelet on my wrist dragging against the water, and I watch my face in the mirror as my hands work automatically.

The water turns a cloudy gray. I drain it, wring the T-shirts out, and bring them back across the hall to my room. I push my clothes to the right side of the rod in my closet to clear a space for them to dry on hangers, and I lay the towel that I took from the linen closet on the floor to collect their drips. I close the closet door and lie down on my bed to wait for Uncle Evan to come in and practice lines with me so I can feel alive again.

☆

The days are endless patterns of darkness, light, darkness, light, darkness, light. One Monday in March, I'm at rehearsal, off-stage, waiting for my cue. It's the last scene of the play, and Zeus is about to take me out of the Underworld. Everything around me is light. I reach up to the zipper on my sweatshirt. I know that as soon as rehearsal is over, the darkness will move in again.

I don't want to let it.

I unzip my sweatshirt. Just a little, an inch, maybe two, and pull my necklace out. I look down at it. The bird reflects the stage lights, and I smile.

"Grayson?" I look to Finn. "Your line, kid," he says, and I walk out to the center of the stage.

☆

When rehearsal is over, Paige comes over to me. I'm leaning over, pulling my jacket out of my backpack, and I can feel the bird dangling on its chain under my neck as I watch her glittery shoes approach. I automatically reach my hand up and touch the charm. I could tuck it back into my sweatshirt, but I can't let the darkness move in again. So I stand up.

"Hey," she says.

I lower my hand. "Hi."

"Oh, cool necklace!" she squeals, and, for a second, she raises her hand to her own necklace—a colorful circle of red and orange glass hanging on a piece of brown leather. "Is that new?"

I straighten out the chain while watching her eyes. I can feel the neckline of my lavender T-shirt behind it. "Thanks, and not really," I say carefully.

She keeps looking at me and reaches her hand out to touch the charm. I feel a gentle tug on the back of my neck. She turns the bird around with her fingers. She studies it. I picture her sparkly, blue fingernails on top of the shining silver, and the lavender T-shirt behind. "So," she finally says. "Is your uncle getting you?"

"Actually, my aunt's supposed to meet me outside. She was at some PTA meeting."

"Cool. I didn't know she was on the PTA."

"Well, she used to be. She quit a while ago, but I guess she's rejoining."

"Should we go?" she asks.

"Yeah, sure." We walk outside. It's not as dark out now at five thirty as it used to be. Spring is coming, but it's still freezing. We stop at the top of the cement steps, and I zip my sweatshirt, put on my jacket, and pull up the hood.

"There's your dad," I say as his car pulls into the drive.

“’Kay. See ya, Grayson.” She slides her mitten along the metal railing as she walks down the steps two at a time. I shove my frozen hands into my pockets.

“Hey, Paige?” I call, and she turns around at the bottom. I’m shivering.

“Yeah?” she asks, pulling her knitted hat farther down over her ears.

I want to say something, but I don’t know what. “Nothing,” I say. “See ya.”

She smiles at me and waves. I sit down on the icy step to wait for Aunt Sally. A few minutes later, she rounds the side of the building, and we walk through the parking lot to her car. “How’s everything, Grayson?” she asks.

“Fine, I guess,” I say, watching my feet trudge through icy snow.

“Anything interesting happen at school?” She digs through her purse for her car keys, her frozen breath hanging in the air between us as she speaks.

I shrug as she unlocks the doors. Part of me wants to hug her and show her my necklace and T-shirt. But a bigger part of me feels like a freak standing there next to her. I get in the car and we ride home in silence.

Chapter 28

THE NEXT MORNING I sit in Humanities and watch the door for Finn. Ryan walks in, and I immediately put my hand up to my neck to cover the bird charm resting against the outside of my sweatshirt. Thankfully, Finn is right behind him. His lips are pushed together tightly, and the look in his eyes reminds me of Uncle Evan when he's stressed out about work. He throws his briefcase onto his chair. It lands with a slap.

"Seats," he yells over us. I watch him carefully, my hand still covering my charm. I've never seen him like this, and a distant memory comes to me in broken pieces. I'm holding a smooth porcelain cat in my tiny hands. A thin, winding crack covers its back, like a gray spiderweb. I feel Mom's presence high above me. A hand reaches down and grabs the cat.

"Silent reading," Finn practically whispers to the now-quiet class. "For the double period." I hear groans. "You can complain all you want," he continues. "I know lots of you are probably behind in *To Kill a Mockingbird*, anyway. And for those of you who aren't, you can reread until you truly understand it."

I look around and see that everyone else is doing the same thing. We've never had silent reading for more than twenty minutes in Humanities, and nobody's ever seen Finn angry about anything. I unzip my backpack quickly and take out my book.

I try to read, but I can't focus. Finn is pacing up and down in front of the board, chewing on a pen. The class is silent except for the sounds of pages turning. The quiet hangs over us like a cloudy sky.

A few minutes before the end of the double period, there's a tap on the door. The whole class looks up quickly. Dr. Shiner is standing in the hallway, glaring through the small, rectangular window. Without saying anything to us, Finn quickly walks out to the hall. As soon as he closes the door behind him, the class explodes into chaos. I look at the clock. The bell is about to ring anyway, so I lean over to zip my book into my backpack. I barely reread a page. When I sit back up, Ryan is standing over my desk. I immediately reach up and touch my bird charm.

"Nice necklace, Gracie," he says. "So." He pauses. "How's it feel?"

"What do you mean?" I ask weakly. I wish Paige were here.

"What I mean, freak, is how does it feel to know that Finn's getting fired because of *you*?"

I stare up at him. The floor starts to shift under me, slowly, like a canyon is about to open up right under the school. The room is becoming too quiet again.

"What are you talking about?" I whisper.

Ryan turns to the row next to us. Everyone is staring. "He doesn't even know!" he says, smirking. "My mom told me your aunt was there," he says. "At the PTA meeting? Man, you are totally clueless."

Suddenly, things are coming together in the too quiet, stale air—puzzle pieces are floating, connecting. *I'm* why Aunt Sally wanted to rejoin the PTA. And so is Finn.

"My mom wouldn't tell me what happened," Ryan continues, "but I'll get it out of her. She tells me and my brother *everything*. All she said was it had something to do with you. My guess? Finn's being booted for making you into a fag like him!" The canyon beneath us is getting wider. Ryan bends down and put his face in front of mine. The bell rings, but nobody moves. "He do something to you, Gracie?" he goes on. The classroom is silent.

My body is frozen and on fire, all at the same time. I think back to that day in the hallway when Paige ran over and saved me. I wish that she were here. I know I could never scream at Ryan like she did, but I don't have to stay here and listen to him. I reach down for my backpack.

There's a rustle next to me, and I look over. Meagan is making her way through the desks. Her face is flushed, and she's looking at the floor. Her thin, black hair is hanging down the sides of her cheeks like black curtains. She stops next to Ryan, in front of me. A second later, Hannah and Hailey are by her side.

Meagan pushes her hair back from her face. "Ready to go, Grayson?" she asks as I throw my backpack over my shoulder. Her voice is quiet, but the room is silent; everyone can hear her.

"Yeah," I whisper. I feel like I'm floating over the floor as the four of us walk to the door. In the hallway, Finn and Dr. Shiner are talking in quick, hushed voices. They stop when we pass by them. I look up at Finn's deep, brown eyes. He looks away.

At rehearsal, everything is different. Dr. Shiner is already in the front row of the auditorium when Paige and I get there, and none of the girls are sitting around gossiping about Meagan and Sebastian. Nobody is passing around a hairbrush or digging a handful of clips out of their backpack.

We join the others on stage, and I hear two seventh graders, Stephanie and Lindsey, whispering something about what Lindsey's mom told her last night. "We should just ask him what's going on," I hear Stephanie say, and my heart skips a beat. I look down at the bird charm hanging against my blue sweatshirt as I sit on the stage between Paige and Meagan to wait for Finn. Paige puts her arm around me. I notice that she's looking right at Dr. Shiner, and the feel of her bony arm over my shoulder makes me want to cry.

Finn finally shows up, and we start rehearsal. I scream

to him silently: *Look at me! Tell me what's happening!* But he doesn't. I can't get the picture of Ryan's stupid face out of my mind. The darkness hangs over the stage, and I think everyone can feel it. I look at Stephanie and Lindsey. They're still whispering to each other.

On stage, Andrew is telling Paige that he's going to help her find Persephone. Paige is supposed to be upset that I'm missing, but I can tell she's distracted. She keeps glancing down at the tattered script in her hands.

Finn is pacing up and down in front of the stage, his hand over his mouth as he watches. When Paige and Andrew finally stumble through to the end of the scene, they look over to him. "Sorry, Finn," Paige says. She fiddles with the script in her hands. He doesn't say anything for a minute.

"You know what, guys?" he finally says. "It's okay. It is okay." He repeats it, looking thoughtful, but it kind of feels like he's talking to himself. "It's a hard scene. And if it's not perfect, it's not the end of the world."

I watch from where I'm standing at the side of the stage, halfway behind the burgundy curtain. I twirl my plastic bracelet slowly around my wrist.

"We'll get it, Finn," Andrew says. "You don't have to worry. We'll both work on it more."

"No, Andrew, don't worry. Like I said, it's a hard scene. Let's just move on, okay? Act Three, Scene Two. Let's do it." He claps his hands together once, and the sound echoes through the auditorium before it drops onto the stage and dies. The massive room is silent. I look at Dr. Shiner. His legs are crossed neatly, and his face is sharp. He's biting his lower lip.

"Come on, Scene Two. Let's do it." Nobody moves, so he says it one more time, and we take our places.

☆

After rehearsal, Uncle Evan's car is waiting for me, and I run down the steps, get in, and slam the door.

"Grayson?" he asks. "What's going on?" But he asks it weakly, like he already knows the answer. I have so much to say, but my mouth won't work. My throat is tight, like my own body is trying to suffocate me.

"Why would she? Finn's the best teacher." It's all I can manage to get out.

Uncle Evan is quiet, and he punches the radio off. I can hear the wind whipping around the car. "Well," he finally begins, "I think she just felt that he overstepped a boundary." I know him, and he's choosing his words carefully. He's protecting her.

"But I want this!" I scream.

"I know, Grayson, I know you do."

"Is it true that Finn's getting fired now?"

"Fired? Oh, I don't think so. I think the question on the table is whether it was within his right to unilaterally make the decision to cast you as Persephone."

I can't talk anymore, so I lean my head back and close my eyes as Uncle Evan pulls out of the parking lot. And the thought suddenly comes to me: what if I quit? I open my eyes and sit forward in my seat. If I quit, would all of this just go away? Uncle Evan looks at me. "You okay, Grayson?"

I don't want to quit. "No," I tell him.

"I know. I'm sorry."

That night, I dream of the Grand Canyon. I'm walking on the rim next to a funnel cloud. It spins wildly next to me. It's so close, and I know it's going to push me in. I can't stop it. I peek into the swirling cloud, and I see my own face staring back at me, my hair arranged into even blond braids.

Chapter 29

EVERYBODY HAS HEARD the rumors. The next morning in Humanities, nobody is talking or laughing. Nobody is sitting on top of anyone else's desk waiting for Finn to tell them to hop off and get to their seats. Everybody thinks Finn is getting fired—all because of me.

I think about what Uncle Evan said in the car. I don't know what's true and what's not. Finn is at the front of the classroom, staring at us like he doesn't know what to do with us.

Across the room from me, Asher waves his hand in the air. "Yes, Asher?" Finn asks. He sounds exhausted. Asher looks at Jason and then back to Finn. My body tenses. I know he's going to ask him what's going on. *Do it!* I scream silently. I can't believe I want him to say it out loud, but I'm dying to know.

But Asher suddenly looks embarrassed. "Never mind, Finn," he says, and Finn nods and looks out the window as he rubs the dark stubble on his cheeks.

"I'm sorry," Finn finally says, looking back at us. "I'm sorry about yesterday. I shouldn't have made you sit for an hour and a half doing silent reading. That was not the right thing to do." He looks like he wants to go on, but he doesn't. He turns his attendance binder around in his hands absently.

"Today, we're going to get back to business. We're going to start working on our debates based on *To Kill a Mockingbird*. For this assignment, I need you in groups of four."

The class is fidgety. Everyone knows what is coming next.

"So," Finn continues, "I can feel your vibe. It's fine. Find your groups and push your four desks together to create small tables. You're going to be sitting here through the end of the quarter." The classroom is getting louder. I watch a truck drive through a pile of slush outside the window. "Once you're sitting with your groups, we'll discuss which themes we should debate. Go ahead. Find your partners."

There's commotion around me—desks and chairs moving, and people finally laughing and talking. But I keep my eyes on my desk. I don't care who I end up with.

"Grayson?" I look up. It's Meagan. "Come on, we saved you a spot." On the other side of the room, in front of the cabinets where Finn stores all the extra books, Hailey's and Hannah's desks are pushed side by side. Meagan's desk is across from Hannah's, and there's an empty space next to it.

"Thanks," I mumble. I pick up my backpack and start to push my chair and desk across the floor. I pass Finn's desk. He's sitting on it, watching the class, fiddling with his pen. I smile at him weakly as I pass by him, but he looks away.

My eyes start to sting. He hates me. Maybe Uncle Evan doesn't know what he's talking about. Maybe I *am* getting Finn fired. Of *course* he hates me.

Amelia and Lila are in the other corner of the room side by side, across from Asher and Jason. They're giggling. Ryan is carrying his chair over his head as he walks from one end of the room to the other. "Come on, Sebastian, just join our group," he's yelling. Sebastian is standing next to Anthony, looking helpless. Finally, he picks up his chair and follows Ryan.

I fit my desk into the open space next to Meagan's just as Finn hops off his desk and starts to weave his way through our clusters, directing us to rearrange this way or that. "I'm looking for six tables of four desks each. Straighten yourselves up! It looks like a tornado swept through here!" He stops in front of Ryan and Sebastian's group and has them all get up and move their desks closer to the windows. When he finally has us the way he wants us, he stands in front of the chalkboard and scribbles *Debate Topics* on the board.

"Notebooks out!" It feels, in this moment, at least, like the real Finn is back. I pick up my gold glitter pen and write the date in my notebook. The outside light bounces off the shimmering writing and it's kind of hard to read, but I don't mind. It makes me forget about the darkness and think about the light.

I try to hold on to this feeling for as long as I can until I look at Ryan across the room and remember everything else.

☆

At rehearsal on Friday, we're all sitting in a clump onstage. Dr. Shiner must have come in during our relaxation exercises. He's in the front row again, watching us. Finn sounds tired, but he is still upbeat as he reminds us that the performance is now less than two weeks away. I rub my burning eyes and look up to the ceiling at the bright stage lights as he talks.

"Please remember, and remind your parents, that a week from tomorrow we're having a Saturday rehearsal," Finn is saying. "Our parent volunteers will be coming in to put the finishing touches on the costumes they made. You can tell your families that I need you at twelve thirty, and I promise to have you out of here by three."

He pauses and looks us over. "We're going to pick back up with the final scene when Zeus escorts Persephone home. Ms. Landen has agreed to help us out here, and we're honored to have her assistance." He glances over to where she's sitting in the second row, kind of hidden by Dr. Shiner. I hadn't even noticed her there, and she smiles and waves at us. I've barely seen her since tryouts.

"As you may know, Ms. Landen has a great deal of experience directing Porter's musicals, and she's going to help us figure out our spacing and timing since, for the last scene, we're going to have the entire cast onstage." He nods at her. "Thanks, Samantha," he says. She gives him a little salute, and we take our places.

I sit next to Andrew in a cardboard horse-drawn carriage. Reid and the Souls of the Underworld are supposed to be on one side of the stage, and Paige and the Elves on the other, but nobody is where they're supposed to be, and Finn is directing people this way and that. It feels like forever before the scene actually starts. But the stage lights are bright. And even though Finn probably hates me, I can't help feeling happy. I'm in the crystal light now.

"Remember where you're standing! Remember who you're supposed to be next to! Keep away from center stage! That's the space that Grayson and Andrew need to use!" Finn yells.

Finally, Ms. Landen steps in. "May I?" I hear her ask Finn.

"By all means," he says, sighing.

"Okay, guys?" she says calmly, and everyone quiets down. "I need to tell you something. I know this feels like chaos now, but I want you all to listen to me." She pauses, and it looks like she's trying to figure out how to put something into words.

Finally, she starts again. "Something I've learned over the years is that often, as the production date approaches, the rehearsals become more and more difficult. I'm not exactly sure why," she continues, "but I have a theory that sometimes, everything needs to fall apart before it can come back together the way it's supposed to." She pauses and looks us over. The room is silent. "Does that make sense to you?" Everyone stares at her.

She looks us over and nods. "You'll see. Just wait. Let's take it from the beginning of this final scene, okay?"

We make it through to the end, and I look to the auditorium seats as Hermes gives his closing monologue. Finn's hand is covering his mouth, and he looks beaten down. He has dark circles under his eyes.

The scene was a complete mess, and no matter what he says, I know he wants it to be perfect. It's the last scene of the play. And it's probably the last play he'll ever direct at Porter, I think to myself.

All because of me.

Chapter 30

I CAN'T STAND the thought of the weekend. A few summers ago at Tessa and Hank's, they put out a raccoon trap next to the opening under the back steps. They stuffed it full of boysenberries and left it out overnight. In the morning, there was a baby raccoon huddled in the corner. The boysenberries were still scattered on the floor of the trap and matted into the baby's stiff fur. Jack, Brett, and I sat there forever on the itchy grass watching it until the guy from Animal Control finally came and took it away. This is what I think about as I lie on my bed after dinner, my wrinkled script in my hand.

I can hear Aunt Sally and Uncle Evan talking in the living room. I can tell they're trying to be quiet, but their voices keep exploding. I creep out of my bedroom and listen to them as they yell in whispers. “I didn’t *mean* for everything to happen like this, okay?” Aunt Sally says.

“Well, what on earth did you expect, Sally?”

“What did I expect? I expected Mr. Finnegan to give Grayson a different role. Or he easily could have just agreed to switch Persephone into a male character—directors do that all the time. At the very least, he could have agreed that Grayson’s costume shouldn’t be a *gown*, for heaven’s sake. All I expected was for everyone to do the right thing—to keep Grayson *safe*. I didn’t expect anyone to talk about *firing* Mr. Finnegan.” Her voice rises as she talks.

“Would you quiet down? And besides, you’re being dramatic. It was a handful of parents who brought up the idea of firing him, not Dr. Shiner.” Uncle Evan pauses, and I imagine him staring out the window. “Regardless,” he goes on, “I wonder if he’ll stick around after this.” For a minute, nobody says anything. “If he leaves Porter, for whatever reason, those certainly are some big shoes to fill. He’s one of the most popular teachers there.”

“Great, that’s great, Evan. Just make me feel as guilty as possible. Anyway, I don’t care about any of that. This is about what’s best for *Grayson*.”

My stomach lurches, and before I know what I’m doing, I step into the living room. Uncle Evan is standing by the window, like I imagined, gazing out over the black lake. Aunt Sally looks up at me and opens her mouth to say something. Then she closes it.

Suddenly, words are flying out of my mouth. “You don’t care

about what's best for me," I say, quietly at first. "I *want* this role." But before I know it, I'm screaming. "Anyway, you think I'm a monster!"

Aunt Sally sits down on the love seat. It looks like she's about to cry. Good. Uncle Evan comes over to me and puts his hand on my shoulder. "Grayson," he says, but he looks at Aunt Sally as he talks, not at me. "Sit down. Of *course* your aunt Sally doesn't think you're a *monster.* You're upset—and rightfully so. You must have a lot of questions."

I look at him through burning tears. "How could someone get fired for giving somebody a role in a play? I wanted that role. I tried out for it!" I scream these last words. I won't sit down. I stare at the two of them.

Uncle Evan finally sits on one of the brown leather chairs across from Aunt Sally. He crosses his legs and uncrosses them, and takes a deep breath. "The question on the table, Grayson, is whether or not Mr. Finnegan acted in line with Porter's philosophy of properly teaching and guiding the whole student."

"What are you talking about?"

"Well, some parents on the PTA," he says, glancing at Aunt Sally, "think it was irresponsible of Mr. Finnegan to give you a role that has, well, implications, without consulting with the administration, the guardians, and the rest of the teaching team."

"But I wanted that role," I scream again. I talk slowly, pausing after each word. "I. Tried. Out. For. It."

For a minute, nobody says anything.

"What are they going to do to him?" I ask, my heart pounding.

"We don't know, Grayson," Uncle Evan says. "There's talk among some parents on the PTA that he should be fired, but Dr. Shiner certainly hasn't said anything about that."

"Could they cancel the play?" I ask quickly.

"I can't imagine they'd do that. But I do imagine they'll at least monitor his theater productions much more closely from now on. I just don't know how it will unfold." He pauses. "It would be a shame for anyone to get in the way of someone who really does have his students' best interests at heart," he continues as he looks over at Aunt Sally.

She stands up, glares at him, and storms out of the living room. I hear the front door of the apartment slam.

Uncle Evan flinches but doesn't say anything about it. I walk down the hallway toward my room. "Grayson," Uncle Evan calls after me, but I keep walking. I can't bear to have him looking at me. I go into my bedroom and slam the door.

At school, Finn acts like nothing's wrong, and I can't understand it. We have the whole double period to work on our debates, and he's writing out the topics and teams on the board. I scream silent messages to him—*Look at me!* But he won't.

I unscrew the top of my gold glitter pen, take out the thin cylinder of ink, lay all its pieces on my desk, and absently put it back together. I glance quickly across the room. Ryan is daydreaming, and Sebastian is waving his hand in the air. Finn finishes writing and turns around. "Yes, Sebastian," he asks, rubbing his stubbly chin.

"Can we switch teams?"

"For what reason?"

"Well, what if we got assigned to debate something we don't agree with?"

Finn looks at Sebastian with heavy eyes, and finally, his face softens. "Something I believe in," he says, looking around the room, "is that it builds character to stand in someone else's shoes. You know, to try to see things from another perspective." He nods, like he's thinking about what he said, but Sebastian just sighs, rests his head in his hand, and looks out the window.

Chapter 31

THE WEEK CRAWLS BY. Every time I walk into Humanities or rehearsal, I expect Finn to pull me aside. I want him to tell me this isn't my fault and explain what's happening. Instead, he acts like everything is fine—like the whole school isn't talking about the fact that he might get fired because of me.

Thankfully, our dress rehearsal is on Saturday, so at least I have an excuse to get away from Aunt Sally. Uncle Evan hardly ever goes to the office on the weekends, but he says he's happy to get some work done there, and he'll drop me off at twelve thirty and pick me up when I call him.

At school, I walk down the quiet, dark hallways. At the entrance to the auditorium, I stop and lean against the door frame. It looks hectic inside. Finn and Ms. Landen are scooting around from person to person. Costumes, most of them only partly finished, are draped over the auditorium seats, and a few parents are sitting behind sewing machines that are set up on a long table in front of the stage. Meagan's mom is in one of the aisles, draping thick red velvet around Andrew's shoulders. I take a deep breath and walk inside. She and Andrew smile at me as I pass them.

Paige hops off the stage and meets me halfway down the aisle. "Hey, Grayson," she says, "You're here! Wanna meet my mom?"

"Yeah, cool," I say. She pulls me up the stage steps. "Do you know if she finished my costume?"

"I think so. The lady loves to sew. She's so bizarre." A woman with an older version of Paige's face is unfolding a huge piece of pink satin in the middle of the stage. I look from Paige's shimmery turquoise leggings, gold scarf, and colorful shirt to her mom's brown corduroys, green sweater, and dark-rimmed glasses. A pin hangs out of the corner of her mouth, and she takes it out as Paige and I approach her.

"Mom, *this* is Grayson," Paige says.

"Hi, Mrs. Francis," I say.

"Grayson, please," she says beaming. "I feel like I already know you—call me Marla." I look at Paige. "I've really enjoyed making your costume," she adds.

"You have?" I ask, smiling back at her.

"Of course I have," she says, nodding. "Very much so." The underneath side of her hair is damp, and she smells like shampoo.

There's a list on the ground, and she picks it up, studies it, and then she looks back to me. "So, Persephone's gown just needs a few final adjustments."

"Great! What do I do?"

"Oh, nothing, sweetie. I have your measurements that you turned in to Mr. Finnegan a while ago, but as long as I'm here, let me just remeasure you. You might have grown in the last month. It'll just take a minute. Take off your jacket."

I do, and I drop it behind the curtain. Paige sits down at her mom's feet. I look from Paige's sparkling silver shoes to her mom's brown suede loafers. "Okay, Grayson," Marla says. She pulls a paper tape measure out of her pocket. "Let's see what we've got." She measures my leg, from hip bone to ankle, and squints at the piece of paper on the ground. "Wow!" she says, smiling. "According to this measurement, you've grown over half an inch in a month!" She measures one more time and eyes the paper again. "Yup," she says. "Growth spurt!"

She gently lifts up my sweatshirt and measures my waist. I close my eyes. My heart is racing now and my chest feels tight, like a rubber band that's being pulled and pulled and is about to snap.

"Okay, honey, let me get your arm and chest measurements. Why don't you take off your sweatshirt?"

I open my eyes. I can see myself reflected in her glasses, and I watch myself as I slowly tuck my hair behind my ears. I don't have a choice. What am I supposed to do, tell her I refuse to take it off? So I watch my hand reach for the zipper, and I shift my gaze to her other lens to watch the sequined heart appear. I drop my sweatshirt onto the floor by my feet.

Beyond her glasses and the hearts, Marla's brown eyes blink gently. Once. Twice. She lifts her hand to my chin, and I think of my bird charm between Paige's fingers. I watch Marla's eyes as she drags the tape measure from my shoulder blade to my wrist bone. When I glance down at Paige, I see that she isn't looking at me. She's looking at her mom.

"I'll do the other arm, too," Marla says. "Just to make sure you're even." She measures my right arm. "Perfect," she says. "Now, lift up your arms a bit. Let me get your chest." She wraps the tape measure around me. It hugs the sequined heart. Tight.

Finn is walking up the stage steps now. I look at his face and I miss how things used to be. I remember standing in front of him on stage, way back in December, asking if I could try out for Persephone. I remember the burgundy curtains and the warm water-air and the first time I held the script. I can't imagine what I must look like to him now, standing on stage in a girl's shirt. I glance behind him to see if anyone else has noticed, but everyone seems busy with something else.

He walks over to us, his eyes fixed on my shirt, and stands in front of me for a minute until, for the first time in weeks, he looks at my face. He looks happy. I realize I've been holding my breath, and, carefully, slowly, I start to breathe again.

He turns to Marla. "Everything going okay?" he asks.

"Samantha and I can't tell you how much we appreciate all you've done."

"Honestly, Brian, I love this kind of project. Paige keeps telling me I'm obsessed with my sewing machine." She laughs a little. "Really, it's my pleasure."

"Well, thank you. It means quite a lot to us to have your help."

"I'm happy to do it," Marla says as Finn walks down the stage steps. He turns around when he gets to the bottom, looks from my shirt to my face one more time, smiles, and walks away.

Marla finishes measuring me, and I look down at my sweatshirt. Nobody is looking at me, and it doesn't seem like anyone else has noticed what I'm wearing. I know Paige won't care. Finn's back is to us. He's searching for Natalie, who is next on Marla's list. I don't know what to do, so I put the sweatshirt back on. I don't zip it, but I wrap it around myself and fold my arms over it to keep it in place.

Natalie hoists herself up onto the stage, and I pull my bird charm out and sit down next to Paige. "I like your shirt," she says, nudging me.

I look at her—at her clothes and scarf that are so different from what other people at Porter wear. "Yeah, thanks," I say.

"I mean, I think it's cool of you to wear something so unique."

I look at my feet. I don't know how to explain to her that she's missing the point, but I smile again, anyway. We sit there, side by side, and watch Marla trim the golden belt on Natalie's lavender robe. It's only a little after one o'clock, and I could call

Uncle Evan to tell him I'm done, but I don't. Paige and I clean up fabric scraps as Marla works, and Paige braids my hair. She talks a lot about Liam and how he asked her to be his science partner. I study her face and her hand gestures and look at her fingers. They're covered in silver rings, and I think of the one I tried on at the Second Hand. I wonder if it's still there.

When Marla is done, we help her fold up the leftover fabric and put it into plastic bags. "Do you need a ride home, Grayson?" she asks me.

"No, thanks," I tell her. "I told my uncle I'd call him when we were done. He's at his office."

"It's no problem for me to drive you," Marla says. "Why don't you call him and tell him we'll drop you off? We could go get something to eat on the way. I'm starving. Are you guys starving?"

"Absolutely!" Paige says. I look from her to her mom, shrug, and smile.

"Great!" Marla says. She looks excited. "Paigey said you live downtown, right?"

Hearing her say "Paigey" makes me imagine a little girl in a diaper and a sparkling T-shirt. I smile to myself. "Yeah, on Randolph," I tell her. "By the lake."

"So, you know where we should go? Paigey, remember that sushi place we went to with the Wilsons last summer? Wasn't that downtown, near Randolph?"

"You want to go for sushi at three o'clock?" Paige asks. She looks at me and rolls her eyes, but Marla is still smiling. I think of Mom's face in the picture on my nightstand. I try to imagine how it would look today, but I can't; I don't know how to. All of a sudden, it feels like the car accident was a million years ago, and I don't know if that's a good or a bad thing.

"Who cares?" Marla asks. "That place was amazing! Where's my phone? I'm going to look it up." She digs through her purse. "Do you need to borrow my phone to call your uncle, Grayson?" she asks.

"No, I've got mine," I tell her.

"Oh, okay."

"Mom, I'm going to the bathroom before we go. Grayson, come with me," Paige says, pulling me off the stage.

"Okay, Paigey," I tell her.

"Watch it." She grins. I hold my unzipped sweatshirt in place, and we walk out the doors of the auditorium together. The hallway is empty and quiet, and I stop walking outside of the auditorium doors as Paige continues across the hall and into the girls' room. "Be right back!" she calls over her shoulder. The light green door closes slowly behind her and clicks into place.

I stand there. I'm frozen.

On the door is a black stick figure in a dress. GIRLS, it says. I want to push the door open and go in with Paige. I want us to stand next to each other at the sinks while we wash our hands and talk about how she thinks Liam is cute. I want to borrow her hairbrush. It's hard to breathe and my heart is thumping, and all of a sudden, I'm worried that it might explode from all these years of *wishing*. I'm worried that it might explode into a million tiny pieces, and that then I'll be gone—invisible again. But this time, for real.

I look around. The hallway is empty, and I walk toward the light green door. I touch the cold metal. I'm so *close* to what I need. But I can't open it. Even Paige would think I'm a freak if I walked into the bathroom with her, so I zip my sweatshirt and go to the boys' room instead. I try to hold on to the feeling of the cool door on my fingertips. I try to breathe carefully so my heart will slow down. I pay attention to the air coming in, the air going out. I go to the bathroom. I wash my hands. I rub my eyes and splash water on my face. In the dirty mirror, my cheeks look flushed. I blot them dry with rough paper towels, and when I come out, Paige and Marla are waiting for me.

In the car, I text Uncle Evan to tell him about the change in plans. I feel shaky as I watch the low, dark sky outside the window. There's a bright circle buried behind the gray. The sun is trying to peek through, but it can't.

The sushi place is empty except for us, and we sit by the window. I fiddle with the white tablecloth that hangs onto my lap as Marla orders us edamame to share. The waitress walks away. "You know," I blurt out, the words forming suddenly in my mouth, "the reason everyone's talking about Finn getting fired is because of me. He'll barely even talk to me anymore." It's a relief to say it out loud. Paige looks to her mom. Marla picks up her chopsticks, snaps them apart, and studies them for a minute.

"Well, Grayson," she finally says, "usually, when it comes to political matters at Porter, I try to stay out of things. But this," she goes on, "well, Paigey and I have spent a lot of time talking about how this is different."

I look at Paige as Marla continues. "I know that there are some parents who want Mr. Finnegan fired because he gave you the role of a female character." She pauses, and it looks like she's trying to decide what to say. The waitress comes and puts a bowl of edamame in the middle of the table. Marla thanks her, and finally, she continues. "Sometimes people make important choices that happen to be risky. I agree with Mr. Finnegan's decision. And I think it was an extremely noble one to make," she says. "Paige and I both do. We've talked a lot about it. And as for him not talking to you . . ." She studies my face carefully. "What do you mean, honey? Are you sure about that? I'd imagine he's just distracted?"

Hearing her words makes me feel better even though I know she's wrong about that last part. But I can't talk about it anymore, so I just shrug. Marla looks out the window and squints a little. "Look," she says, "the sun is finally peeking through!" She turns back and smiles at me. "Let's order a bunch of things to share, okay?"

"Okay," I say. I watch her hair fall to the sides of her face as she studies the menu for us, and I wonder again about Mom, and how she'd look if she were sitting here with us, too. Then I think again of how weird it is to miss someone I can barely even remember. Across the table from me, Paige squeezes her edamame until the bean pops out. It lands in my glass of water, and I laugh.

☆

When we pull up in front of my building, I thank Marla for the sushi and the ride. I want to say more, but I don't know how to put what I'm feeling into words. I look at Paige as she sits in the passenger seat and adjusts the gold, silky scarf around her neck.

"So, I'll see you Monday," I say to her.

"Sounds good."

"Grayson," Marla says, "I just have to say—we want you to know that you are welcome at our house anytime you need anything. *Anytime*."

"Mom!" Paige says rolling her eyes. "Why do you have to be such a drama queen?" But she's smiling.

"I'm sorry, I'm sorry. I know. I can't help it." She looks back at me as I climb out of the car. "But I mean it, Grayson."

"Thanks," I say. I mean it, too.

Chapter 32

THE PLAY IS ONLY three days away. When Paige and I walk into the auditorium after school on Monday, the crew kids, a few of the moms, Finn, and Ms. Landen are already there. This is the first day in forever that Finn hasn't been late, and he and Ms. Landen are standing next to two science lab carts piled high with colorful, flowing costumes. I scour the fabrics with my eyes until I find the golden gown Marla made for me.

Paige and I jump onto the stage. Finn looks our way, says something to Ms. Landen, and walks over to us. When he stops in front of me, I smile at him weakly, and this time he doesn't look away.

"Grayson, do you have a minute?" he asks. I can't make my mouth work, but I nod. He motions for me to follow him, and I jump down. Everything is a blur. We walk over to the side of the auditorium. I notice the dark circles under his eyes again, and I'm suddenly embarrassed. I can't believe what I've done to him.

"Grayson," he says, looking around quickly, "I'm going to make this brief because a while ago I agreed to a request from Dr. Shiner that I not spend one-on-one time with you."

"What?" I interrupt.

"I'm not really at the liberty to talk to you about it in detail, so all I'll say is that Dr. Shiner and I made an agreement, and I wanted to be able to continue directing this play." He glances around the auditorium again. "I've probably already said too much," he adds carefully.

I look at his eyes, and he looks down at the paper clip he's been turning around and around in his hand. *This* is why he hasn't said a word to me in weeks? I feel my heart is beating in my throat. And suddenly, Ryan's words pound in my ears: *He do something to you, Gracie?* I feel like breaking something. I feel like crying.

"I'm sorry, Grayson," Finn continues. "I just want you to know that this outcome is not what I intended when I told you that you could try out for Persephone."

"I know," I say. "Of course I know that."

He looks relieved. "If it's okay with you, I'm going to talk frankly with the cast today about my future here at Porter. There are lots of questions swirling, and I feel that people deserve to know what's going on." He pauses and looks at me carefully. "I know you're aware of the rumors. I'm not going to mention anything about you," he continues. "I'm just going to tell everyone what's happening with me. I wanted to make sure you were okay with that. I want you to know that I am aware of how this affects you, too."

I can't say anything. I just nod. I glance over to the stage where everyone is gathered. They're watching us, and the auditorium is too quiet. This is what I've been hoping for, to know the truth, and now I feel like I'm on trial and the jury is about to deliver my verdict.

"Listen, you better go join everyone else." Finn looks to the auditorium doors. Dr. Shiner is walking in. But he doesn't shoo me away. He turns back to me slowly. Deliberately. "I'm sorry, Grayson."

"No, I'm sorr—" I start to say, but he cuts me off.

"No," he says, and points his finger at me. "You have nothing to apologize for. Remember that. Now go join your group." I walk back to the rest of the cast. I don't want to, but I don't know what else to do. I feel too weak to jump up and sit next to Paige again, so I slide down onto the floor alone and lean my back against the wooden cabinets that line the front of the stage.

Everyone is already silent, but Finn asks us for our attention anyway. My heart won't stop pounding, and I look up to where he's standing right in front of me. "Cast and crew," he says, "this is it. This is our last week of rehearsal before the big performance. You all have worked so hard, and I know this is going to be an amazing show. This afternoon, we are doing the performance in full costume. The crew is here, and we need to give them all a big round of applause. They designed and created all the scenery, and they're going to be working the curtains as well as the lights, and doing the scene changes. Without them, there would be no show." Everyone claps. I sit on my hands. Finn looks like a giant from down here, and I focus on the brown leather of his shoes. The soles look worn out.

He pauses. "There's one other order of business that I want to talk to you about before we take our places and begin." He looks us over and glances down at me for a second. I hold my breath and focus on his feet. He continues. "Many of you have probably been wondering about all the rumors swirling around this production for the past few weeks. I believe that rumors are unhealthy. You deserve to know the truth."

The room is still. I look at Dr. Shiner sitting in the front row. His fingertips are pressed together, and he's watching the back of Finn's head as he talks. I look at Finn's feet again as he continues.

"I've made a decision," Finn finally says. "It will soon be time for me to move on." I suddenly feel like I'm in a dark tunnel. Finn's shoes are being sucked away from me by a giant vacuum until I'm on one end and he's on the other. Everything between us is narrow and black.

He goes on. I squeeze my eyes shut and listen. "I've been a teacher at Porter for almost ten years now. Recently, I've been in touch with a small playhouse in New York City called the Central. It's actually a very historic, famous theater. Their current assistant director will be leaving soon, and I'm going to take over her position. It's an amazing job at an amazing theater, and it's something that I can't pass up. So *The Myth of Persephone* will be my last production here at Porter. I feel honored to have gotten to work with all of you on it."

I look away. The tunnel is gone, and all that is left is me, sitting on the floor for everyone to see. *What about me?* I want to scream.

For a split second, Finn looks down at me again. Everyone above me seems frozen, like they're glued in place. "Okay. Places! This is a dress rehearsal. Give it all you've got." His words ring through the silent auditorium.

I stand up in front of him. I can feel the stillness behind me. Slowly, it bleeds into chaos, like someone turning the volume up on the radio. There's whispering, then shouting, then scrambling for costumes. "Grayson," Finn says, taking a step closer to me, "I believe that you can do this without me." He pauses, and then continues. "All of this."

I nod and float backstage. I don't make eye contact with anybody. Ms. Landen helps me step into my golden gown for Act One. And even though Finn is leaving because of it, and even though Aunt Sally thinks I'm a monster, when I look at myself in the giant, floor-to-ceiling mirrors, I finally see myself the way I'm *supposed* to be—my inside self matched up with my outside self. And now, everyone else will finally see it, too.

Chapter 33

IT'S LIKE I'VE been waiting my entire life for this day. The brushstrokes surround me—the bright crystal and the darkness. Tonight I will be a girl in front of an audience. I'm supposed to be a girl, and tonight I will be. And Finn will leave Porter because of it. White and black. Light and dark. And me, in the middle of it all. Gray.

There's nothing else for me to do but walk through these columns of dark and light, so I do; I go through them to the library after fourth period. I have my lunch in my backpack, but there's no way I'll be able to eat it. I have a science project due tomorrow, too. I'm almost done, but I don't know how I'll be able to concentrate enough to finish it. My script is in my backpack, and I smile when I think of it. It's beaten up and worn out, and the cover is taped on now.

"Gracie!"

I don't know why I turn around. In front of me, the late morning light slants through the hall windows. It paints bright rectangles on the tile floor. Next to the rectangles are Ryan and Tyler. And, off to the side, a few steps away, is Jack.

I want to crack open and scramble out of my body. I want to become a bird again and fly up to the ceiling, but I'm stuck on the ground. My eyes are glued to my cousin, and all I can think of is the secret knock I used to use to get into his room—*tap, tap, bang, bang, bang*. Ryan starts to talk, and I shift my eyes away from Jack, onto him.

"You ignoring us, Gracie?" he asks.

"No," I say. It's all I can think of.

"You gonna blow us off again? Why didn't you answer us?"

I shrug.

Tyler's voice now: "You're looking pretty today. Where are you going?"

"Library."

Darkness, Light, Darkness, Light, Darkness, Light.

"Why don't you come with us to the lunchroom? We wanna hang out with you."

Tyler and Ryan are next to me now. Jack hasn't moved, and Tyler looks at him. He claws at him with his eyes, but Jack takes a little step back. Tyler's hand is on my arm now. Ryan grins next to him.

"I'm sorry," Jack suddenly says, and he reaches his hand toward us awkwardly. I don't know who he's talking to. I think of him reaching for my hand at the Grand Canyon. I remember the feel of his palms, callused from baseball practice.

My heartbeat feels like it's coming from outside of me again.

I break free and run through the empty hallway to the staircase. My feet pound another beat on the floor, and my heartbeat and all the footsteps bounce like millions of bullets inside my head.

At the top of the empty staircase, I turn around. Tyler and Ryan are right behind me, and Jack's back is disappearing down the hallway. I feel somebody's hands on my backpack, pulling and then pushing. I steady myself. Hands grab at my hair. I shake my backpack off, and it falls onto the stairs. Someone's feet are under mine now, in between mine, and I feel the hands—pushing again. I grab for the railing, but it's too far away and I'm falling.

First, my forehead. My wrist explodes into flames. Then my knee. Slower now. Finally, the ceiling.

There's no other movement on the stairs, and I turn my head away, toward the open lunchroom door. As I stare into the lunchroom, the first thing I notice is the unbelievable level of noise. Then, I feel the floor pounding. Footsteps are coming my way. I don't try to sit up. I don't want to.

Sebastian's face is suddenly above me. A second later, Dr. Shiner's. "I told you to hurry," Sebastian whispers.

"Thank you, Sebastian," Dr. Shiner sighs.

More pounding. High heels.

Mrs. Nance is kneeling next to me now. Behind her are faces. They lean in toward me, over her shoulders, like weeds.

"Back to the lunchroom!" Dr. Shiner yells.

They disappear, flattened by a tornado. I blink. There's a sharp fire burning in my left wrist.

Mrs. Nance holds something to my forehead. She moves it away. It looks like red paint.

Dr. Shiner kneels down next to me. "Who?" he sputters.

"I already told you what Ryan said." A voice from behind.

The back of Shiner's head. "Didn't I tell everyone to get back to the lunchroom, Sebastian?"

More burning. Flames in my bone.

Mrs. Nance's hand is behind my back now. "It's enough, Ed. I'm taking him to my office. You can ask your questions later."

I'm dizzy when I stand up, and she keeps her hand on my back. My left hand hangs at my side, numb, burning, lifeless.

In the nurse's office, I lie on a cot and look at the tiny black holes on the ceiling tiles. I hear Mrs. Nance in the other room on the phone.

"I'm terribly sorry, Mrs. Sender. He's resting now. Yes, of course. Dr. Shiner's investigating. Well, it is quite swollen. Definitely. It needs to be checked out. Okay. We'll be here. See you soon."

I close my eyes, and I see the aura of reminds me of the spotlights, and I push my with my good hand. "Mrs. Nance?" I call.

Her head appears in the doorway. "Yes, h You really need to take it easy."

"The play's tonight." The darkness is trying to

"I know, dear."

I don't want to let it. "I'm still doing it."

"Lie down, honey. We'll figure it out."

I'm dizzy anyway, so I listen to her.

Finally, I hear Aunt Sally's voice. Why couldn't M have called Uncle Evan? I turn away from her when s in. "Grayson," she says, rushing to my side. She leans o but I keep my eyes on the windows. She walks around other side of the cot and lowers her face until it's next to "Grayson, honey. Are you okay?" The rims of her eyes are "Oh, Grayson. This is *exactly* what I was worried about."

"Mrs. Sender?"

"Yes, what is it, Mrs. Nance?"

"I think he's been through a lot."

"Of course he has." She turns to me. "Your uncle is meeting us at the ER. Do you need help getting up?"

I don't, and I follow her out the door. Mrs. Nance squeezes my good hand as I go.

☆

le Evan meets us outside the front doors to the emergency
m. It's humid out, and the snow is melting off the roof. A
er of dirty water runs along the curb. Uncle Evan and I walk
while Aunt Sally parks the car. I feel like I'm floating, so I sit
wn in the waiting room while Uncle Evan talks to the recep-
onist. I don't want to see anything else that's going on around
ne, so I study the blue-and-white tile floor. I smell rubbing alcohol and hear commotion. I don't look up.

It takes forever to get the X-ray. I sit between Uncle Evan and Aunt Sally while we wait. "I'm still doing the play," I say once, but Uncle Evan tells me to just concentrate on relaxing.

"We'll figure it out," he says.

☆

In the X-ray room, I'm alone with a nurse and a giant, humming metal machine. I catch a glimpse of my wrist. It's pink and swollen, so I look away at a painting of a robin on the wall.

We get to wait in a different room now. A white curtain surrounds a cot, and I lie on it while Aunt Sally and Uncle Evan sit in blue chairs, whispering. Finally, I hear the screeching of metal and a doctor pushes the curtain open.

"Grayson?" she asks, looking down at a clipboard in her hand.

"Yes." Aunt Sally answers for me.

"Good afternoon. I'm Dr. Mitchell," she says, and extends her hand to Aunt Sally, and then Uncle Evan.

"Sally and Evan Sender," Aunt Sally replies. "Is it broken?"

"Well, it's not broken, but it is fractured." She slides the X-ray films out of an envelope and onto the flat, rectangular light on the wall. I look away as she flips the switch. "We call it a hairline fracture. Here it is—you can see it. It's not too bad, as far as fractures go, but he'll need to be in a cast for about two months."

"Jesus," Aunt Sally whispers.

"It could have been a lot worse," the doctor assures her. "What happened, now?" she asks, turning to me. "You fell down the stairs at school?"

I nod.

She studies me, and nobody says anything. "Okay. Well, I'm going to have Allison prepare the plaster for your cast. I'll be back in a few minutes." She walks out.

I look at Aunt Sally and Uncle Evan. "Are you in pain?" Uncle Evan finally asks.

Just then, the curtains open again and a nurse with short, blond hair comes in. "Grayson, right?" she asks, smiling. "I'm going to be helping Dr. Mitchell with the plaster. You want a fancy color for the cast?" She's talking to me like I'm four. I stare at her.

"What's it gonna be, big guy? We've got black, blue—"

"Pink," I say.

"Oh, Grayson," Aunt Sally sighs. "That is just what landed us here in the first place! *Why* would you want a pink cast?"

"Sally!" Uncle Evan hisses it like a warning. "Would you step outside with me for a moment?" He looks at Allison. "Excuse us, please. Grayson can choose whatever color he'd like." The metal rings on the curtains scream as they leave. I can hear their hushed voices coming from the other side. I look at Allison and try to focus on her face. I concentrate on her slightly shifting contact lenses. She studies me.

"So, pink?" she asks. I nod. "Okeydokey." She disappears and I'm alone.

I rest my head on my right hand. Aunt Sally and Uncle Evan's voices have gotten louder.

"Why, after everything that just happened, would we allow him to walk into school with a pink cast on his wrist?" Aunt Sally is saying.

Uncle Evan says something I can't hear, and then nobody says anything. "Well," Uncle Evan finally whispers, "I think I better call Mr. Finnegan."

"Mr. Finnegan? How about Dr. Shiner?"

"We need to discuss what's going to happen tonight, with the play."

Allison comes back in. Dr. Mitchell is a step behind her. She glances back at Aunt Sally and Uncle Evan, and then looks me over.

"Dr. Mitchell?" I ask.

"Yes?" Her eyes are soft and brown.

"I'm the lead in our spring play tonight."

"Hmm." She looks thoughtful. Aunt Sally and Uncle Evan are still yelling at each other in loud whispers.

I'm so sleepy, but I don't want to let the blackness seep into the light places. I feel like a tired soldier. "I need to be in it."

She doesn't say anything for a minute. "I hear you," she finally says.

"Can you tell them it's okay?"

"I'll tell them. As long as you promise to rest up and take it easy after it's done."

I nod. "Thank you," I whisper. I look away. I feel their hands on my arm, on my hand. My wrist is freezing, then hot, wet and then dry. In the end, they say they're done. I finally look down. My hand is resting peacefully by my side, my fracture enclosed in a hard, pink shell.

Chapter 34

The Myth of Persephone

Prologue:

Programs rustling, whispers in the dark
Suddenly: silence
A circle of light frames a messenger
White robe, golden wings
He talks of things
Like good guys, bad guys
And heroes who win
When the curtains slowly rise
Creaking, crawling
And light floods the stage
We stare

Act I, Scene I:

Because inside the costume waits the boy
Who everyone's talking about
Leaning forward, ready
Pink cast swollen on his wrist
His golden gown glows under overhead lights
We smirk
As he frolics through his cardboard garden
(Tiger lilies, willow trees)
Somebody should take that boy for a haircut

Act I, Scene II:

We know backstage
That teacher is guiding, directing
It's like the circus came to town, a freak show
In the still dark
We watch the bright stage
Hades's black robe flows
As he ponders the wanting, the abduction, the capture
Of light

Act I, Scene III:

It's funny, we have to admit
The boy looks graceful up there
His face smooth and calm
His voice a clear bell
When he's whisked away to Hades

The cardboard horses dragging
The sturdy silver carriage
His gown a glorious golden circle around him
We hope he'll jump out: *Run away!*
We scream in our heads
We start to forget he's a boy

Act II, Scene I:

Trapped in the Underworld
Tied down by evil Souls
Persephone watches, helpless
Demeter tears through wilting gardens
Nature dies in her wake
Willows wither, flowers droop, dead leaves
Fall
They fall and they carpet the earth

Act II, Scene II:

In the Underworld, Hades paces
Explains to the Souls
Who hold Persephone down
That they will guard her
Keep her
Forever in the Underworld
But together we smile in the dark
On her face, we see objection
In her eyes, we sense protest

We sit forward in our seats, all at once
Flowers blown forward by a breeze
We want the good guy to win

Act II, Scene III:

We glance side to side at one another
As Persephone drifts through black cardboard trees
The plastic Spring of Lethe
The Underworld
We are:
The little kids, the moms, the dads, the sisters
The brothers
The girl, red hair, the man, red beard
We are:
The grandmas and grandpas from out of town
Kleenex in our pockets, glasses around our necks
We are:
Everyone, in different shades of white and brown

Act III, Scene I:

We are one
We are squinting to see
We are the judges
When Zeus approaches Demeter
Royal, noble, deep red cape
An offer to help in his mighty hands
We clap

Act III, Scene II:

In the Underworld

The girl winces, just once

She rubs her hand over her cast

Surprised it's there

When she lingers at the bench

Absently plucks some fruit off a tree

We know what's coming

We brace ourselves

Act III, Scene III:

Good guys are supposed to win

But she only wins halfway

She'll live six months in light

Six months in darkness

Light

Darkness

Light

Darkness

Light

Lights from behind

Light up the stage

Everyone surrounds her now

The Souls, the Elves, the poor kids who didn't get bigger roles

They're staggered, a wall

Like soldiers

Surrounding the girl
Who rides her carriage home

Epilogue:

In the end the deep-red curtain billows and drops
Lights off, sightless night, still
Then, the spotlight again
A beam of sunlight through crystal
The girl walks out cradling her arm
She must be in pain
The door to the parking lot is open next to the stage and
She feels the humid wind that's holding her up and
She takes her director's hand while
He bows and she curtsies
Gracefully.

Chapter 35

BY THE END of spring break, my wrist doesn't throb anymore, but I'm still not used to the cast. My light blue, long-sleeved T-shirt sticks to it as I pull it on with my right hand. I stand for a minute, looking out my bedroom window at the treetops below, and I adjust my pink T-shirt underneath the blue one the best I can. My charm is resting against my shirt, a silver bird flying against a light blue sky.

Uncle Evan drops Brett off at the elementary school doors and then drives Jack and me over to the circle driveway. We walk through the double doors together and down the hallway.

Ryan won't be in Humanities. Dr. Shiner came to talk to us over break. From my bedroom, I listened to the muffled sounds of adult voices around the dining room table. After more than an hour, Uncle Evan asked me to come out and sit down with them.

"So, Grayson," Uncle Evan had said, all the while staring at Dr. Shiner with sharp eyes, "Ryan has been switched to the other sixth-grade section, per our request. Dr. Shiner has assured us that your paths will cross very infrequently. And Grayson can count on that, Dr. Shiner?" he had asked.

"He can," Dr. Shiner nodded, looking at his hands instead of at me. "Both Ryan and Tyler are prohibited from setting foot anywhere near you again. As you know, they're suspended until the week after break. Once they return, one slipup, and they'll be expelled."

"Sound okay, Grayson?" Uncle Evan had asked me anxiously.

I nodded.

"And, Grayson," Dr. Shiner had gone on, still looking away, "are you sure you don't have anything to add to your statement? Ryan and Tyler *jointly* chased you down the hallway and *jointly* pushed you down the stairs?"

I looked down the hallway. Jack's bedroom door was opened a crack. "I'm sure."

☆

The hallways at school are bustling. "See you after school," Jack says to me when I stop at my locker outside of Finn's door. He carefully looks around at the crowded hallway for a minute. I don't know what to think about him, and I watch his back as he disappears around the corner into the seventh-grade wing.

The idea of taking the bus home instead of going to play practice is the most depressing thought in the world. I wonder what next year's play will be and who will direct it. I take my books out of my locker, load them carefully into my backpack, and walk into the classroom with my head down.

When I get to my seat, I finally look up. Everyone is standing around, talking in strange whispers, and my heart jumps. I follow Meagan's gaze to the front of the room, to where Dr. Shiner is watching us out of the corner of his eye as he hands a young teacher a stack of binders and overflowing manila folders. She is nodding intently as he talks to her.

Finn has left us. I stumble into my seat.

Meagan sits down next to me, but I can't look at her. My throat is dry, and my heart thumps. When the bell rings, Dr. Shiner walks out the door and closes it behind him.

The class explodes into laughter and shouting, but I can barely hear a thing other than the sound of flames roaring in my ears. He didn't even finish the year. He didn't even say good-bye.

Numbly, I watch the new teacher. She walks in front of Finn's desk and looks us over. A paper airplane sails through the air. Some people are sitting in the wrong seats, and Jason and Asher are still sitting on top of their desks.

"I'd like your attention, please," the new teacher says. Her voice is solid and she actually looks calm, like her day is going as planned. She keeps talking, even though only some of us are paying attention.

"When I told my husband that I was going to take a long-term subbing position in a sixth-grade Humanities class, he told me I was nuts." The class is getting quieter now. I hear a few giggles. "I asked him why he would say such a thing," she continues. Everyone has switched back into the right seats now. "He said that sixth graders are animals! I told him I wholeheartedly disagreed with that. Sixth graders are people. So, he wished me luck and told me to embark upon this job at my own risk." She pauses and flashes a big smile. Her teeth are even and white. "And here I am."

I look around as I rub my arm above my cast. "My name is Amber LaBelle," she continues. She turns and writes it on the board—her first name, too. Her handwriting is nothing like Finn's. The letters are neat and solid.

She faces us again, looking serious now. "I know that you are probably confused. It is my understanding that it's a surprise to you that your teacher is not here. I'm sorry to say that I don't know much about the situation. I do know, however, that he left me extremely extensive notes about your current unit." She holds up a thick binder, and then opens it to the first page. She studies it for a minute while we all watch her.

"According to Mr. Finnegan's instructions, we are going to have a discussion today on some of the major themes that you all identified before break in *To Kill a Mockingbird*. This is, I must add, one of my all-time favorite books." She smiles and looks back down at the binder. She bites at her bottom lip as she reads something. "And it seems like we have some big debates to present tomorrow," she finally adds. She looks up again. Her eyes are dark blue, like deep water, and the sound of the flames roaring in my ears is gone now.

She turns and faces the board. I look at her brown leather cowboy boots and her long purple skirt. *Bravery*, she writes on the board to the right of her name. She turns back around and faces us.

"Okay, let's take our notebooks out!" There's a sudden rustling in the classroom. I lean over and take out my notebook and *To Kill a Mockingbird*. "So, tell us, who is brave in this book? Who isn't?" she asks. The class is silent. "Well, don't be shy! What do you all believe the author was trying to tell us about bravery?" More silence. Finally, a few hands wave in the air.

"Thank you! Finally!" Mrs. LaBelle throws her head back and laughs. Her long curls bounce. "Tell me your name before you speak," she says, her voice still bubbling. She points to the back of the classroom.

"Sebastian." I turn quickly and look.

"Okay, Sebastian, go ahead."

"Well, I think to be brave, you have to be scared at the same time. To be brave means there's something important you have to do and you're scared, but you do it anyway." I think of his face, peering out at me from behind Dr. Shiner as I lay at the bottom of the staircase, my wrist in flames. "That's all," he says.

Mrs. LaBelle studies Sebastian thoughtfully for a minute. "Okay, very good." She writes on the board, *Take important action despite fear.*

I listen and take notes. I look up to the clock. It's eight fifty-three, which means nine fifty-three in New York. I look out the window and wonder what Finn is doing now.

Chapter 36

AT HOME THAT NIGHT, Uncle Evan comes into my room after dinner. I've been at my desk, staring at my science textbook for so long that I can barely even see the words anymore. "Hey, Grayson," he says as he sits on my bed. "So, Aunt Sally tells me you said everything was uneventful on your first day back?"

I know what he's getting at. "Yeah, I don't think I have to worry about anyone else." I look down. The TV is on in the other room now, and Aunt Sally is asking Jack if he finished his homework.

"And everything else was okay?" Uncle Evan asks.

"Yeah," I say as I reach up and touch my charm. "Finn's gone."

"Well." It looks like he wants to say something, but he doesn't say anything else. The silence ticks in my ears like a clock.

Finally, he stands up, takes his wallet out of his back pocket, and opens it up. He pulls out two tickets and sits back down. "Today at work Henry asked me if I could use two tickets to the Shakespeare Theater this coming weekend. He and his wife are going out of town. Aunt Sally's not particularly interested in Shakespeare, so she thought maybe you and I could go. It's *Romeo and Juliet*—it's a matinee on Saturday."

I smile at him and nod. "I've heard it's great," I say.

"Yeah? You heard about this? You know, it doesn't surprise me that you're becoming interested in theater. Your parents both loved this kind of thing."

"They did?" I ask.

"Sure." Uncle Evan looks around my room, almost like he's seeing it for the first time. "You know," he says, "when we were kids, your dad and I did absolutely everything together. We were best friends." I didn't know that. "As we grew up, though, I guess we had our own lives, our own paths."

I nod.

"My biggest regret in life . . ." He takes his glasses off and rubs his face. "My biggest regret in life is that we didn't talk much as adults. Your aunt and I got married, your dad and your mom got married. We grew apart." He puts his glasses back on. "It kind of reminds me of you and Jack sometimes." I look down at my hands in my lap. "Your parents loved each other very much, you know," he adds.

"I know."

"They loved you."

"Yeah."

"So, Grayson, there's something that came for you in the mail last week," he says, standing up and opening his wallet again. "Aunt Sally didn't . . . Well, I think your aunt is still searching for a way to process things. I felt, well, I feel that this belongs to you."

The only letters that have ever meant anything to me are the ones from Mom. For the tiniest, split second, I feel like Uncle Evan is about to pull out another letter from her. But I know this is ridiculous. I glance at the painting on my wall as Uncle Evan takes a white envelope out of his wallet. It's folded in half and kind of molded into the shape of the wallet. The return address says *Brian Finnegan.* It's from New York.

"It's from Finn," I say.

"I know." He pauses. "Well, I'll leave you alone," he says. It looks like he wants to say something else, but he doesn't. He gets up, walks out of my room, and closes the door carefully behind him.

I stare at the envelope for a long time. I know that as soon as I read what he wrote, I'm going to forgive Finn for leaving, and I sit and let myself feel furious for another minute. Then, I can't wait any longer, and I carefully rip it open.

March 18

Dear Grayson,

You were amazing in the play tonight, and I'm so proud of you. An old acting teacher of mine in college used to say that "risk taking is free." He was so wrong. It's not free. You took a risk, and now I'm sure you're contending with everything in its wake. Risk taking is not free, but I can assure you, it's worth it.

Grayson, I'm sorry I wasn't up-front with you about when I'd be leaving for New York, and I'm sorry I left without saying good-bye. I guess I was just dealing with too many of my own emotions to do the right thing.

I know it may feel like there are people who are against you, but I want you to remember that most people in the world are good. Look for the people who extend a hand to you. And when they do, take it.

I'm so proud of what you've done this year. And always remember, Grayson, to be brave.

Fondly,
Mr. Finnegan

I read the letter three more times before I put it in my top desk drawer with my letters from Mom. I wish Finn were still here. I'm tired of people leaving me, and I'm tired of the letters they leave behind. I don't want to be left behind anymore.

The next morning in Humanities, I roll my gold glitter pen back and forth between my fingers. Someone has cracked a window open, and a warm, damp breeze is weaving its way through the classroom. The air feels heavy. The world outside is green-gray. It's about to pour.

"We're almost ready for the first debate!" Mrs. LaBelle announces as everyone settles into their seats and quiets down. "Let me see . . ." She leans over the desk and looks at Finn's binder. "Grayson, Hannah, Meagan, Hailey, Ryan, Sebastian, Steven, and Bart. Are you guys ready?" She looks up.

"Ryan switched classes," a voice calls out.

"Ah, that's right." Her face flushes, and she pauses for a minute. "Not a problem," she finally says. "Everyone else, find your note cards and come on up. Does everyone else have a notebook out? I want you all to make sure you're taking extensive notes on each debate. I'm not sure if Mr. Finnegan told you, but you're each going to be choosing one of these topics to write a paper on."

The class groans. Mrs. LaBelle grins. "And, they'll be due at the end of next week. I can't wait to read them!"

Thunder rumbles outside the windows, and the wind is picking up now. Everyone whispers and points at the swaying trees. I dig through my backpack for my note cards. The wind gusts again, and the poems and stories that Finn tacked to the bulletin boards suddenly rustle and jump like they're trying to escape from the wall. Amelia closes the window next to her, and they settle back into place.

I find my note cards in my folder and think again about what Finn said in his letter. Then I think about how Marla called him *noble*, and for some reason, I think about what Ms. Landen said about how, sometimes, everything needs to fall apart before it can come back together the way it's supposed to.

"Okay, what are you waiting for? Group one, come on up!" Mrs. LaBelle says, opening her grade book.

"I can't find my note cards," Bart announces, and Steven and Sebastian get up to help him dig through his backpack. I look past them to where Amelia is sitting next to Lila. Her eyes meet mine. She starts mouthing something, and I turn away. I don't want her to think I'm eavesdropping on whatever she's trying to tell Meagan, Hannah, or Hailey. I look at them, wondering what they're talking to Amelia about across the room. They're all looking through their note cards, though, and I look back at Amelia. She's saying something to *me*. I squint at her lips.

Good. Job. In. The. Play. She smiles. Behind her the rain is starting to slam against the windows. I smile back.

"I think my note cards are in my locker," Bart says to Mrs. LaBelle.

"All right, then, go take a look," she says as the thunder booms again. Everyone squeals.

I turn my note cards around in my hands, and I think about Jack. We didn't say much to each other over break. He seemed kind of quiet, actually. Part of me wanted to talk to him. Part of me wanted to ask him why he left the hallway on the day of the play, but I didn't. I think about it again—his hand held out awkwardly before he ran off. I thought about it all break; I tried to figure out what it meant.

I see his hand in my mind again as he reached for my wrist

that day at the Grand Canyon. I remember the feel of his palms, callused from baseball practice, and his startled smile as he pulled me away from the edge. I see him walking a step ahead of me to the park across the street, his skinny ankles disappearing into his gym shoes. He's standing over the kitchen sink, eating wet raspberries out of a colander. He's handing me a red pillow from his bed to reinforce our fort. He's clutching the slippery side of the sailboat. Lake water is running off of his hair and into his eyes in tiny rivers. He's laughing. He's reaching through the warm water for my hand. I raise my hand.

"Yes? Grayson?" Mrs. LaBelle says.

"Can I go to the bathroom?" I ask.

"Of course you can. Just hurry."

I get up and duck out of the classroom. There's nobody in the hall but me, and I can hear voices coming from behind the closed classroom doors. Name tags hang crookedly above some of the lockers, though lots of them fell off months ago. I stop in front of the drinking fountain. Water is dripping from the bottom of it into a dirty, yellow bucket. I stand there. I listen to the quiet noises around me.

In front of me are the two bathroom doors, and I look back and forth, from one sign to the other. BOYS and GIRLS. I remember Paige's back disappearing into the girls' room across from the auditorium, and my wish fills me again like a fire.

I walk into the boys' room. It's empty. The urinals are disgusting, and they smell like pee. I pass them quickly and go into a stall. It's hard to do it with my cast on, but I peel off my gray thermal and then my pink T-shirt with the sequined heart on it. I'm freezing, and my hands are kind of shaky. I hold my pink T-shirt between my knees and put the thermal back on and then put my forearms into the body of my T-shirt to stretch it out a little. The dried plaster of my cast catches on the T-shirt as I pull it over the thermal. I look down.

I walk out of the stall and stand in front of the tall, dirty mirror that looks like it's about a million years old. There are smudges of rust on it, in the corners and around the edges, and someone has scribbled all over it with a green Sharpie. I think of all the years that I spent wearing boys' clothes and pretending that I looked like I do right now, and I think about how I wished and pretended that everyone else could see me the way I'm supposed to be, the way I *really* am. I take the two tiny hairclips that I've been carrying around out of my pocket and arrange them neatly behind my ears. I smooth out my hair and walk out the doorway and into the hall.

The door to the classroom is closed. I stand in front of it for a minute and look through the window. Bart is holding his note cards now, and he, Sebastian, Steven, Meagan, Hannah, and Hailey are next to Finn's desk. They're talking and laughing with Mrs. LaBelle. They're waiting for me.

I look down at the doorknob. I'm scared, but I do it anyway—I open the door and walk inside.

Acknowledgments

ENDLESS GRATITUDE . . .

To my early readers who expressed enthusiasm and took the time to talk to me and ask me important questions. Your excitement upon reading (some *very* unpolished) drafts of this book kept me moving forward. Joyce Heyman, Laura Bleill, Christy O'Brien, Dale Lipschultz, GraceAnne DeCandido, and Lisa Pliscou—thank you for embracing me and Grayson early on in my journey.

To my fellow workshoppers at StoryStudio Chicago for being present at the start and providing thoughtful, much-needed feedback.

To Molly Backes for your generous gifts of time and insight. Thank you for giving me the confidence to call myself a writer.

To Caryn Fliegler, my oldest friend and trusted reader—you read multiple drafts and gave me invaluable feedback from day one. Thank you for looking out for Grayson and telling me once that nothing should matter but the experiences she was created to endure.

To Lydia Polonsky for being my first editor, Kenneth Polonsky for your feedback and excitement, and the entire Polonsky clan for eagerly anticipating each new stage with me.

To Susan Caruso for giving me days upon days to write and for your insights into the life of a drama geek. Thank you for your never-ending support of me as a parent, writer, and person.

To my parents for your unflagging enthusiasm about my writing career and for your all-around backing during this new phase of my life: Barbara Hurwitz, thank you for many things, but especially for being my number one fan. Martin Lipschultz, thank you for teaching me to always look for the gray. And to Dan Lipschultz, thank you for being my childhood partner in observation, analysis, and crime.

To my trusted agent, Wendy Schmalz, for taking me and Grayson under your wing with such quick enthusiasm that I am still pinching myself. Thank you for always being there to answer my many questions and to support me as a writer and a human being.

To my talented editor, Lisa Yoskowitz, for believing in Grayson and paving the path for her entry into the world. I am

Acknowledgments

ENDLESS GRATITUDE . . .

To my early readers who expressed enthusiasm and took the time to talk to me and ask me important questions. Your excitement upon reading (some *very* unpolished) drafts of this book kept me moving forward. Joyce Heyman, Laura Bleill, Christy O'Brien, Dale Lipschultz, GraceAnne DeCandido, and Lisa Pliscou—thank you for embracing me and Grayson early on in my journey.

To my fellow workshoppers at StoryStudio Chicago for being present at the start and providing thoughtful, much-needed feedback.

To Molly Backes for your generous gifts of time and insight. Thank you for giving me the confidence to call myself a writer.

To Caryn Fliegler, my oldest friend and trusted reader—you read multiple drafts and gave me invaluable feedback from day one. Thank you for looking out for Grayson and telling me once that nothing should matter but the experiences she was created to endure.

To Lydia Polonsky for being my first editor, Kenneth Polonsky for your feedback and excitement, and the entire Polonsky clan for eagerly anticipating each new stage with me.

To Susan Caruso for giving me days upon days to write and for your insights into the life of a drama geek. Thank you for your never-ending support of me as a parent, writer, and person.

To my parents for your unflagging enthusiasm about my writing career and for your all-around backing during this new phase of my life: Barbara Hurwitz, thank you for many things, but especially for being my number one fan. Martin Lipschultz, thank you for teaching me to always look for the gray. And to Dan Lipschultz, thank you for being my childhood partner in observation, analysis, and crime.

To my trusted agent, Wendy Schmalz, for taking me and Grayson under your wing with such quick enthusiasm that I am still pinching myself. Thank you for always being there to answer my many questions and to support me as a writer and a human being.

To my talented editor, Lisa Yoskowitz, for believing in Grayson and paving the path for her entry into the world. I am forever grateful for the questions you asked and for your help in making this book what it is now. And to the entire team at Hyperion, especially Suzanne Murphy, Stephanie Lurie, Dina Sherman, Liz Usuriello, and Julie Moody—thank you for your important contributions and amazing support.

And, finally, to my family, the inspiration for everything: Benny, who is all love and only light; Ella, my sensitive, fierce, and brave little friend; and Daniel, my first reader and first love.